DAWN OF DELIVERANCE

DAWN OF DELIVERANCE

A NEW DAWN™ BOOK THREE

AMY HOPKINS

MICHAEL ANDERLE

DISRUPTIVE IMAGINATION®

From Amy

This book would not have been written, if not for the hard work and dedication from the people working at the Peanut M&M's factory. Their talent at crafting the perfect nut-to-chocolate ratio, combined with just the right amount of hard shell crunch, will not be forgotten.

From Michael

To Family, Friends and
Those Who Love To Read.
May We All Enjoy Grace
To Live The Life We AreCalled.

CHAPTER ONE

Danil clung to the tree, wondering how the hell he had let himself get talked into this idiocy.

"Sharne, jump!" Jakob yelled.

Sharne jumped, her effort buoyed by Jakob's magic. She shot into the air, and the hog dashed under her and slammed into a tree.

Not just any tree. The trunk Danil gripped shuddered and groaned at the impact. When it stilled, he was sure it was no longer entirely upright.

Through Garrett's eyes, he watched the rearick chase down a fat sow, his feet flying as he jumped over bushes and thick tree roots.

He saw Bette, panting behind a tree as she took a moment to catch her breath before swinging around to fire off another round from her crossbow.

Then, he felt Carey's urgent spike of fear as a nearby tree trunk split, the old pine leaning precariously to one side.

Oh, Danil realized. *That's why it feels like I'm falling.*

Danil screamed as the tree lurched towards the ground. The

sudden shift in his center of gravity pulled him away from the trunk, and his hands stung as he lost grip on his refuge.

He screamed again as he fell, falling into a whimper as Jakob's magic caught him and lowered him gently to the ground.

Then, he screamed louder again as Jakob and Sharne both suddenly realized what would happen next.

The hog eyed him. Steam shot from his snout as he snorted in the cold morning air, one foot stamping on the ground menacingly.

"Danil!" Sharne screamed.

"Duck!" Bette yelled.

Unsure who she had been talking to, everyone threw themselves to the ground—everyone but Danil, who was already there, his borrowed sight flitting between his companions before settling to watch the red eyeballs of his impending death.

The hog's left eye exploded in a shower of blood.

It screamed and gasped, pulling back in a brief moment of agony before falling to one side, dead.

"Take that, ye hairy side of bacon!" Garrett yelled triumphantly in the distance.

Bette strode over and pulled Danil to his feet. He stood, knees shaking.

"There, now," she said with a grin. "Wasn't that fun? Ye should come out huntin' fer breakfast more often, mystic!"

CHAPTER TWO

Julianne carried the tray of loaves into the town hall, carefully stepping over the piled up clothes at the doorway. Her foot caught in a fold of cloth, and she stumbled into a heavyset man who caught her, saving both her dignity and the food.

"Thank you," Julianne said. She tried to read his mind to grab his name, but his shield was strong.

"Couldn't have that food on the floor," the man chuckled. "I'm starving!"

"Sorry, love!" Tansy called out, making her way free of the cluster of people around her. "Those clothes are waiting to go out to wash. I'll pick 'em up right quick."

The tiny woman pranced over to Julianne, dressed in a black leotard and sparkling cat ears perched on her head and waving her long hair for maximum benefit to the men watching her. She stopped to inhale the fresh rolls before she scooped up the pile of clothes. "Smells delish!"

Peeking around the side of the enormous pile, she walked with Julianne. "Any word on Adeline? Old George is missing her something fierce."

"I don't know anything you don't," Julianne said. "I'm sorry, Tansy. I know you guys really care about her."

Tansy shrugged, the movement threatening to topple the stack of laundry. "She's a clever kid, knows how to look after herself." She paused, then said, "Hey, Julianne? Thanks for taking us in. I mean it—we ran from Muir with our tails between our legs. If not for you guys…"

"It's not me you need to thank," Julianne told her with a shake of her head. "You're not the only ones the people of Than have accepted without question."

Tansy nodded in understanding, dropping the clothes in a corner.

"Harlon's bringing down some meat and eggs," Julianne said. "Is there somewhere where I can put it down?"

"Over here, Julianne!" Madam Seher called out. She stood by a makeshift table, crafted from an old door resting on a frame Francis had put together from scrap wood. "Oh, thank you, dear. Just what we needed."

"Harlon?" Julianne set down her tray, then waved over the people in the hall to attract his attention as he walked in. "Over here!"

Harlon was mindful as he shuffled through, careful to keep his precious platter steady and away from the curious faces that turned to sniff the wafting aroma of sausages and steak.

"Here you go." He set it down, staring at the food longingly.

"Go on, Harlon," Julianne said with a laugh. "Grab something for the walk back to your ma's."

He grinned like an eager child, then dug his thumbs into a bread roll and tore it in half. Slipping a juicy steak inside, he bowed to Julianne before ambling off.

"How is he?" Seher asked.

"Good, thanks to you." Julianne touched the old woman's arm. "I mean it… a few weeks ago, he barely left his room and wouldn't speak to anyone. Whatever healing spell you used has made a huge difference."

She'd shrugged off Julianne's words. "It was nothing."

"You gave him back his life," Julianne said."

"You've done enough for us," Seher reminded Julianne. "It was time I paid a little back."

"Stop nattering, old woman." Tansy thrust a plate at Madam Seher. "Last time the Tahn's brought food, you were so busy feeding us that you forgot to eat. Don't you even *think* I didn't notice!"

"I'll leave you be, so you can eat." Julianne shoved some food on a plate and scooted away before Madam Seher could protest. "Bye!" She waved at Tansy, who wrinkled her nose and wiggled her fingers in farewell.

Heading out of the hall and across the street, Julianne knocked on a freshly painted red door. When she had first seen it, the door had been a soft sky blue. Now, any semblance of that color—the color worn by the New Dawn—had been scrubbed off or painted away.

"Lord George?" Julianne called tentatively.

"Eh? Who's that?" From behind the door, Julianne heard the floorboards creaking and a moment later, the curtains twitched before the door swung open a man with a cane greeted her.

"Young Julianne!" Lord George beamed, his smile widening when his eyes dropped to see what was in her hands. "Oh, I say," he shuffled back to let her in, watching the food as she went by. "You've bought breakfast!"

Julianne pointed toward his leg as he came into the dining area. "How's the leg doing?"

"Oh, it's well enough I suppose." His wince of pain as he sat showed the lie in his words.

She bit her tongue and tried to keep a smile on her face. He was a proud man that many depended on, and wouldn't show weakness if he could help it. "Did you bring some for yourself?" he asked, and clicked his tongue when she shook her head.

"I ate at home," she explained.

"Not the point, not the point at all. You're going to sit there and watch me? Well, at least sit down and pour yourself a drink, so I don't feel like a glutton." Lord George patted the seat next to him.

Julianne stepped through the room into the tiny kitchen. He didn't really need one—the villagers had fawned over him, delivering meals and checking in multiple times per day to see if he needed anything. She brought the water pitcher back with two ceramic cups.

"Here," she said. "I got you one, too."

"How is that rabble in the hall? Not making a mess, I hope. I did ask them to quiet down, but you know what those theatre types are like."

"Never having met a 'theatre type', I didn't really know anything at all!" Julianne exclaimed.

George sat up a little. "What have they been doing?"

A slow grin spread across Julianne's face as she remembered some of the antics she had seen since they had arrived in town. "Well, I swear Tansy must own at least a dozen cat costumes. Every time she goes out, there's a gaggle of children around her."

"Not taking them from their schooling or work, I hope?" George said seriously.

Julianne laughed. "Their parents are just glad they aren't underfoot. Some of the girls have found little ears to wear, or have scarves tucked into their skirts like tails."

"You almost sound jealous," Lord George said, settling back into his chair.

Julianne blushed. "I wouldn't be the only adult in town who loves to see the cartwheels and twirls in the middle of the streets. Even their illusions are different to what I'm used to—they use their magic purely for fun. It's a nice change."

"Glad to see you having fun, dear," George said with a smile. "But you weren't smiling when you came in. Is everything ok?"

Julianne sighed, reality tumbling back in to wash away thoughts of performers in the street. "Everything is fine. I'm just thinking over all the things I have to do today."

"Ahh, of course. The curse of leadership. Always busy, always another thing to do and another problem to solve. You don't need to humor an old thing like me. Go on, off you go." He ushered her off the chair.

"Don't be silly, this is the only moment of peace I get in the morning!" She leaned down to peck him on the cheek. "I adore our breakfasts together." Still, she let him herd her out the door, mindful of the long list of things that needed her attention.

George patted her arm and thanked her for delivering him the food. "And if you have trouble with that rabble outside, you just let me know. I'll pull them into line."

Julianne knew that 'pull them into line' would involve a few kind words, and the entire 'rabble' falling over themselves to accommodate his wishes. Though far from perfect, Lord George had done his best to run Muir well.

He had introduced free schooling for the poor, and the itinerant travelers that often passed through the town. A free kitchen run by the local clergy—shut down after the New Dawn had sunk their claws in—provided food to those without money, and to the workers leaving home early or returning late after a long day at work.

"Goodbye, George," Julianne called, shutting the door behind her. The steady thump of wood on floorboards faded as he made his way back to his chair, cane at his side.

Now, where the bloody hell is Danil? Julianne wondered. She sent out a general probe, hoping he was in town. *Ahh, there you are.*

Help! he sent back, alarm clear in his thoughts. *I'm being accosted by an angry hooker!*

CHAPTER THREE

What did you do to deserve that? Julianne managed to convey the mental version of a stern look and a raised eyebrow with the thought.

What? Why would you even assume that? His response was more indignant than alarmed, so Julianne wasn't too worried.

I'm coming, she sent, hiding her laughter.

She hurried over to the schoolroom, a little abandoned house that had been commandeered to teach the local Tahn villagers the basics of mental shielding. Classes had been lacking the last two weeks, as the villagers and the mystics teaching them had all become too busy to keep up.

Now, Danil was using it as his own place to sleep upstairs, while taking any official meetings with the people from Tahn and Muir downstairs.

He sent her a quick scatter of thoughts to show her what he was dealing with. Julianne was surprised to see Polly, a prostitute from Muir, arguing with him.

Polly had been in town a week, but Julianne hadn't had the chance to speak to her—not that she had a reason to. Julianne had met the girl, but she had wiped her mind after the encounter, so she wouldn't know Julianne from a bar of soap.

"It's a *perfectly* acceptable occupation!" Polly was yelling as Julianne arrived.

"I never said it wasn't! But right here, right now, is *not* the place to start your little enterprise." Danil flung the door open to let Julianne in, his face set into a scowl and flushed from the argument. "*You* explain it to her. She won't listen to *me*."

Julianne grabbed the collar of his robe as he slipped past, and dragged him back inside. "You're not getting out of it that easily. Sit." She pointed to a seat and he took it, glowering at the girl who now stood over him.

"You, too," Julianne said.

Polly turned up her nose. "I don't have to do a damned thing you—eek!" She sat, looking about in alarm as her body seemed to move of its own will. As she caught Julianne's eyes fading from white back to their normal color, she snarled.

"You're not a dog," Julianne said pleasantly. "Use your words. Kindly, or I'll *make* you."

Grinding her teeth, Polly sat in silence. Danil spoke up instead. "Polly here thinks the middle of a war is the perfect time to set up a brothel in Tahn."

"That's sound reasoning," Julianne commented.

Danil's face fell. "You can't be serious!"

"I didn't say it would necessarily work," she added. "Polly, have you thought it through?"

"What's there to think about?" she quipped, shooting Danil a triumphant smirk. "I've got two or three girls from the Friendship with me. All we need is a soft bed and a place to hang a sign."

"*Friendship*? Is that what you call it there?" Danil snorted.

Julianne whacked the back of his head. "Behave, before I make you."

He paled and slouched low in his chair. "Sorry, Master."

"Where will you find a soft bed? Under the stars? We don't

have enough housing to accommodate the people in town now, how do you think you'll find a clean place to work from?" Julianne asked Polly.

"I— uhh, I..." Polly stammered, looking around the room for inspiration. "I'll buy a house! I have coins with me. I don't imagine a place would cost much *here*." She said the last word with derision, and Julianne read her poor opinion of the town in her mind.

"This is a town that works on a barter system. Most of the residents don't have money—they don't need it. How will you and your girls make a living?" Julianne asked.

Polly lost her righteous indignation, her confident smile slipping away. "No money?" she asked.

Julianne pressed on. "Do your friends even *want* to return to their old profession? We're in desperate need of cooks, clothiers, and gardeners, to name a few. Even someone who didn't want to work a profession could be happy here, simply by providing for themselves and trading what they can for the rest."

Polly looked away, scrambling for an answer.

"And if you *do* intend to employ these girls, you will have a responsibility to provide for them. We can't be feeding people who are lying around waiting for work, when there's so much to do." Julianne rested her hands on her hips, waiting for Polly's reply.

"So, the answer is no, then?" Polly snapped.

"The *answer* is that it's not up to me. You'll have to come up with a proposal of your own, address the foreseeable issues— only half of which I've covered, mind you—and present that to the town council for approval."

Slumping in defeat, Polly blew her cheeks out. "It's impossible."

Julianne touched her shoulder. "*Anything* is possible if you set your mind to it. You just have to make sure it's what you really want and what your girls want. Madam Nacht might have been your dream when you thought that's all there was, but you've stepped into a place where possibility doesn't end."

Polly's eyes popped open wide. "How did you know?" she whispered. Madam Nacht was the name she had told Julianne she would take if she had the chance to start her own brothel, in a new city to the north.

Of course, Polly had thought Julianne was a man—a rich, arrogant noble just out for a good time, and was forgotten the moment he left the building.

"Just don't rush into it," Julianne told her. "Good things come to those who work hard, plan smart, and make friends." She looked from Polly to Danil, hoping the girl got the hint—alienating the people here wouldn't do her any favors.

Polly nodded. "Fine. I guess you have a point." She stood, brushed down her skirts and walked out.

"I can't believe you're encouraging her," Danil snapped as soon as she had left.

"I thought out of everyone here, you'd be in *favor* of the idea," Julianne said. "You've never been a prude before."

"I have no problem with her setting up business once things settle down," he said. "What pisses me off is someone who walks into a situation and immediately decides they can profit from it."

"And was that her genuine intention?" Julianne asked softly.

Danil blushed. "I don't know."

Julianne didn't say anything, just watched him roll the question around his head.

"*Fine*, I was too angry to look any deeper. I saw what she wanted to ask me, and I reacted. Are you happy?"

"Oh, Danil," Julianne said with a laugh. "I'm not trying to berate you."

"No," he said. "But the fact that I'm right ninety-nine percent of the time must mean you get a little joy the one time I'm not." He grinned and bowed when she shook her head in exasperation. "Hey, it's not easy being perfect."

"Bitch, help me, What am I going to do with you?" Julianne asked.

"I'd say you could take me over your knee and spank me, but you'd best save that for lover boy."

"Oh, you… you…" Unable to find words to express her feelings, she satisfied herself by slapping him upside the head, going for a second one when he ducked the first. "You're *incorrigible!*" she finally gasped.

"Like I said, it's not easy being perfect! Anyway, back to the topic at hand: We have a hall full of refugees—very flexible refugees, but refugees nonetheless—and we're harboring a kidnapped lord. Do we have a plan to deal with this yet?"

Collapsing into a chair, Julianne groaned. "No. I can't get Madam Seher to agree to help. She hasn't said no, but she keeps asking us to wait until Adeline makes it out." Worry cast a shadow on Julianne's face. "Danil, it's been two weeks. What if she's already dead?"

"Why don't we just go get her?" he asked, as though he were suggesting a trip to the market for a loaf of bread.

"Right. We'll just sneak into a fortress full of mystics who can shield the shit out of each other, steal the princess from the tower, and escape with our hides intact."

"That's a great plan!" Danil said without a hint of irony. He plucked an apple from a nearby bowl and sank his teeth into it with a loud *crunch.* "Who are we taking?"

"It's too dangerous." Julianne ran a hand through her hair, doing her best to keep her frustration behind a thick mental shield.

"Never stopped you before." Danil threw a second apple at Julianne, who caught it one-handed.

"He'll be expecting us. He knows what I can do, and he'll be prepared." She rolled the apple in her hands, thinking.

"He's lost his general and half an army. What *did* happen to young George, by the way?"

"I let him go," Julianne said with a deep sigh. "His mind was so full of holes that when I took his body over, I broke a few things in the process. He'll be wandering the countryside somewhere, hopefully with enough wits left to shelter from the animals and the cold."

"You don't think he's a danger?" Danil asked, concern etched on his features.

Julianne's doubt about letting him go resurfaced, and she chewed at her lip before answering. "Perhaps. But I don't know that he's entirely at fault for what happened, and the damage he's suffered is enough punishment for what he did do." She shrugged, knowing she would make the same choice again if she had to. "I don't think he'll come back, though. He was pretty scared when I left him."

Scared was an understatement. George Junior had been cowering in a ball, rocking back and forth while he whimpered to himself, shaking and trembling. He had wet himself, too, though he didn't give any indication that he had realized it.

"Fair enough." Ever loyal, Danil took her word that George's errant son wouldn't be back to cause trouble.

"You're right about the rest, though," Julianne said, still mulling over his comment from earlier. Rogan *had* sustained a heavy blow by losing the lord's son and his army. If they waited too long, that small advantage would be lost.

"I am?" Danil asked, confused.

"We need to move, and soon." She looked around the small, cluttered room. "Can we set up a meeting here? For tonight?"

Danil nodded. "I can make some space."

"You don't have a class scheduled? I don't want to interrupt if you do."

"No," Danil said. "Most of the villagers can either shield well enough to practice on their own, or they'll never pick it up, so I've stopped the classes until things settle down."

"That's fine, but I intend to start them up again," Julianne said.

"I don't want people getting lazy. It's the only defense they have against the muckers."

Danil looked surprised at her use of the word 'mucker', a shortened version of the phrase 'mind fucker'. The villagers had only used the word in reference to those who had abused their power.

They made plans for the evening meeting and Julianne left to go about her day. She needed to organize the food stores, giving the village a chance to stock up before winter. The hogs the soldiers caught would replenish their food for a little while, but they needed more than just meat to last them through the colder months.

After that, she would need to track down the people she wanted at the meeting, check the guard rotations were going well, make sure the small army they were amassing had enough armor and weapons...

"I'm tired just thinking about it," she said aloud. Still, the thought of finally making a plan to end this war sent frissons of electricity down her spine in a combination of nerves and excitement.

CHAPTER FOUR

Adeline sat at the end of her bed, back straight and muscles tense, listening to the ravings of a madman.

"So, my dear daughter, I have decided to act. No longer can my enemies be allowed to undermine my rule. The townspeople are angry, angry at these insurgents and what they have done."

"What will you do, Father?" she asked, swallowing bile at the false words.

This man was not her father. Her *real* father was stowed away safely in a small village somewhere. This man? He was an imposter, a trickster using mental magic to disguise himself as the gentle Lord George.

"I will smite them," the man hissed. "I will crush them like weevils and feed their bones to the dogs. No one—*no one*—can be allowed to stand against me, to thwart my power like they have."

Adeline was certain the man was Rogan. The leader of the New Dawn had wiped her memory each time she had seen him, and for a long time, she had wondered if she was simply going crazy and he didn't exist at all.

After confirming his presence with others, though, and

recording the smallest remembered snippets of her encounters with him, she was quite sure this was him.

Like many in a position of power, Rogan hadn't thought that lowly commoners and prostitutes were worth mind-wiping. Adeline had gone to great lengths to speak to the forgotten people of the city, catching scraps of information and vague rumors about the man who stood as her father's advisor.

Rogan was known to be petulant and impulsive. He was easy to enrage and offend, and violent when the mood took him. He didn't inflict physical punishment himself, but twice now, a person in the street had been subjected to an invisible flogging, writhing around the cobbled road and screaming in pain.

The local brothel told of a man who walked in and demanded service, which the lady of the house had been magically compelled to provide. The two girls that had gone in never came out. It was rumored that he had killed them, but no one was sure.

Adeline knew.

They were in the dungeons below her father's castle, the building that served as his home, as the town offices, and below, as its prison.

She'd snuck down once, aching to see who was kept down there. She'd seen the cell her father had been kept in, his rumpled jacket still on the floor in one corner. Next to it, two girls sat on dirty straw, staring at the wall.

Adeline had crept away before being seen, returning the stolen keys so that no one would know of her little trip.

She had enlisted Jill, one of her maids, to sneak food down for the girls on a regular basis. As one of the few of George's staff who had been taught to shield her mind like Adeline, she was about the only person left in Muir who could be trusted.

Jill had barely been seen in the past week, and not at all for two days.

Adeline hoped Jill was ok and that the girls were still alive.

For the last week, she had been locked in her room, guarded closely by the two new soldiers lurking in the hall.

"There is something else I must tell you about." Rogan's demeanor suddenly changed, becoming nervous, shy.

"Perhaps it could wait?" Adeline tried to dodge the conversation she had assumed was coming her way. "I didn't sleep well, Father. I'm terribly tired."

He ignored her protest, not that she was surprised. "Rogan is a fine man. Terribly smart and so benevolent to my—to *our* —people."

Adeline stared at the floor, muscle in her jaw flexing. *How dare he use my father for this*, she thought to herself. Her thoughts might be safe behind a mental shield, but she needed to work harder to control her physical reaction.

"I do think you'd like him," Rogan continued. "And you're getting old, too old to be without a husband."

Adeline didn't respond. Her heart thundered in her chest, and her white hands gripped her skirts so tight she knew it would be wrinkled when she stood.

Since confining her to her room, Rogan had spent more and more time with her, masquerading as Lord George. Somehow, he had grown to have some kind of twisted affection for his prisoner.

Adeline knew she would have to find a way to use it against him, but the thought of being forced into marriage with the man who was trying to take her city left little room for a clear head.

"I tire of this," Rogan said. He often ended his visits abruptly, and Adeline suspected it was his magic, exhausting him after long days spent maintaining the magical illusion. "Goodbye, my dear daughter. Think on what I said about Rogan."

"Of course, father."

Adeline braced herself, and forced a smile as he leaned down to kiss her forehead. *He doesn't even smell like father*, she thought, glad her innate shield had so far prevented him from reading her mind.

He left and shut the door behind him. She fled across her room on tiptoes and pressed her ear to the door. As she listened, one hand fished a long chain from between her breasts, and took out a thin, silver key.

"...back tomorrow," he was saying to the guards.

"Yes, Master," they answered in unison.

Their words suggested they were loyal to Rogan, who had insisted his title was Master. He had never said *what* he was a master of.

She listened as the hard click of boots on the stone floor faded away, locked the door with a quiet *click*, then ran to her bed. She stuffed her pillows beneath the blankets in the rough shape of a sleeping body, then ran to a small writing desk against the wall. She penned a quick letter on a tiny scrap of paper.

Rogan more unstable. Threatening to come for you.

She didn't mention his burgeoning crush. Madam Seher wouldn't stand for that and would rush in to rescue her without thinking. It was too early for that, and would risk any plans they might come up with.

With one last look at the door to make sure it was shut tightly, Adeline dove under her desk. It took a moment of groping the hard stone to find the tiny crack and slip her fingers in. With a low grating sound, the hidden door opened.

She crawled in, then stood in the hidden cavity behind the wall. A lever on this side closed the hidden door, and a peephole disguised by a tapestry in the room would give her a chance to make sure the room was empty before she returned.

Now, though, she had a job to do.

A narrow staircase led up to one of the old towers. The only other entrance was boarded up, a precaution Lord George had taken after some klutz of a cleaner had fallen from the tower. In such a peaceful region, he had lamented the mere presence of them before blocking them off.

Adeline's little door was the only way in, as far as she knew. She had discovered it as a child, and never told a soul. Now, it was literally a lifesaver.

"Percival?" she called softly as she neared the top of the stairs. "Are you still here?" She had meant to come up at dawn, but Rogan's unscheduled visit had almost caught her out.

Flapping wings rustled behind her, and she greeted the pigeon with a small curtsy. "Thank you for waiting, Percival." He chirped, then hopped onto her hand, cooing happily as she stroked his grey feathers.

"You know the drill. I'll try to be gentle, but if you flap around like last time, you'll just make it more difficult."

The bird couldn't understand a word she said, but seemed soothed by her words. Adeline rolled up her message into a tight little scroll, and used a bit of string to tie it to the bird's foot.

"There. Mathias will be looking for you," Adeline whispered.

At her gesture, the bird launched himself out of her hands and into the air, gliding away from the tower and into the sky.

Adeline watched until he was no more than a speck, then took a careful peek at the city below. It was quieter than usual, residents herded off the streets by a newly formed city Guard.

This group of soldiers, employed by Rogan, were rougher and meaner than her father's men. They had strong armed one of the inns into closing, and almost killed business at the other two with strictly enforced curfews and harsh punishments for anyone seen drunk in the streets.

"Just you wait, you bastard," she whispered. "You'll pay for ruining our city. Just you wait."

CHAPTER FIVE

Bette rubbed her shirt on the washboard, humming loudly.

"I haven't heard that tune," Tansy said next to her.

"No? Well, that's because it's a rearick song; somethin' we sing up at Craigston," Bette explained.

"Where's that?" Tansy asked.

Bette lowered her voice dramatically. "It's across the Madlands! Ye have to brave the crazed beast-men, then travel through the low-lying valley. Just when yer feet are ready ta fall off, ye come ta the biggest, nastiest mountain ye ever laid eyes upon!"

Tansy's own eyes were wide, lapping up the story.

"Once ye start climbin', the air gets real thin. Yer lungs get tight, and the air gets colder and colder, until yer walkin' through a blizzard. Only then will ye find a wee shinin' light in the snow and sleet, a little twinkle to guide ye ta Craigston, where the mountain people hail from."

"And a few miles up from that, us weak-kneed, soft-bellied mystics live," Bastian threw in. He squeezed out a wet pair of pants, then dunked them into the stream again. "It's really not *that* bad."

"Bastian, ye bloody spoilsport. I was tellin' a story!" Bette slapped him with her shirt, splattering him with water.

"Hey, this is my only clean outfit!" he protested. "Then you should wash your clothes more often," Tansy chided him. "Though, I suppose I should be glad you wash them at all. Bette, how'd you teach these dumb lugs to look after themselves?"

"Teach them?" Bette asked. "I near bloody drowned the last one who thought I'd be his washer-woman."

"If not for Julianne, Garrett would still be stuck head-first in a water barrel," Bastian confirmed. "Believe me, *no* man would ask Julianne or Bette to do their laundry. Not if you value your balls."

He tossed his wrung-out clothes in a basket, then swung it over his shoulder. "Catch you ladies later," he called, nodding respectfully to Polly as she passed him on his way out.

Polly threw herself on the ground, dumping a heavy basket of clothes beside her. Her eyes were red and puffy, and her mouth set in a tight line.

"You alright there, Pol?" Tansy asked cautiously.

"I'm fine," Polly snapped.

Bette shrugged, willing to let the girl be, but Tansy wouldn't let it go.

"You are not; you've been crying. Did one of our boys do something? If he did, I'll box his ears."

Polly gave a quick shake of her head and Tansy sat back down. "Oh. Pity, I could've done with a tousle. What is it, then?"

"It's everything!" Polly threw her hands up in despair, fresh tears dripping down her face. "When Jakob came to tell me I had to leave Muir, I was terrified. Everything I had, I've left behind—friends, family, my home."

Tansy reached a wet hand out to pat Polly's shoulder awkwardly. "You'll be 'right, now. Once we clear those bastards outta Muir, we'll all be able to go home."

"Home to what?" Polly snapped. "I've lost my job and half the town thinks I'm a traitor." She glowered at Tansy. "It's alright for you lot. You'll get to be involved in the big battle, people will see you saving their asses. Not me. I'll be stuck in this pig shit of a town."

"What's that rubbish, then?" Bette exclaimed. "Ye don't intend ta help us take down Rogan?"

Polly snorted. "As if anyone would let a dirty hooker get involved. The only thing I'm good at is fucking things, and I'm not even allowed to do that anymore. Well, not for money, at least. And if I'm not getting paid, what's the point?"

Bette's eyes widened. "Do ye think the people of Tahn here were born with weapons in their hands or shields on their minds? They've worked bloody hard to recover, and to grow strong enough ter fight back."

Polly raised her face from her hands, eyeing Bette warily. "You think I could learn to fight?" she asked, sniffling.

"Anyone can learn ta hold a pointy stick and shove it up a man's arse," Bette said, wagging a finger. "But a woman that's learned where the rest of his soft bits are is likely to have a few tricks of her own. Yer saying it's not so?"

Polly sighed and flopped back on the grass, tears dry now that her mind worked over what Bette said. "I can get out of a grapple or a headlock, and I know where to stick a dagger in close quarters, if that's what you mean."

"Aye, exactly! Now I just have ta teach ye ta do it from a little farther away."

"I can help!" Tansy cried. "I used to do a sword swallowing act. Have you ever tried to dance while swinging four blades, with another one down your throat?"

"Well, I've had to dance with something down my throat, but it wasn't a sword," Polly quipped.

"I'd rather the sword!" Tansy squealed.

"So, would I," Polly agreed, finally cracking a smile.

Bette hooted and slapped the ground. "Aye, lassie, you'll train up quick, I'll bet. If ye wanna see just how fast, well, all ye can do is see for yerself."

"Ok, then," Polly said, sitting up. "I'll show that uptight, mystic bastard I can be good for something. He'll see."

"And which uptight mystic bastard might we be talkin' about?" Bette asked, curiosity piqued by the passion on Polly's face.

"Danil." The word hissed out between clenched teeth.

"Oh, aye. He'll see something, alright," Bette murmured to herself.

A fury like Polly's could only come from one place—she cared what Danil thought of her, and he had given her the impression that it wasn't much.

"This'll be fun," Tansy commented after Polly had gathered her skirts and left, promising to come and see Bette for her first training lesson in the morning. "Poor old Danil won't know what hit him."

CHAPTER SIX

That evening, Lord George and Madam Seher arrived at Danil's for dinner together.

"Good evening!" Lord George looked around the small cottage approvingly. It was sparsely furnished and even less decorated.

George understood the young mystic had no sight, though he would never have guessed unless he had been told. He assumed bulky furniture would make it hard to navigate the small rooms, and that decorations would just be wasted on a resident who couldn't see.

"Is Julianne attending this evening?" Madam Seher asked.

George saw her eyes flash white and cleared his throat politely. "I do understand, Seher, it must be a joy to find someone to use your incredible magic with; but please remember, I can't read your mind, or anyone else's?"

She laughed, apologizing and quickly explaining that Danil had told her—through mental words—that Julianne was on her way, and the soldier, Marcus, would be with her. "I'll try to remember to use my words while you're here, George."

"Don't apologise, I do understand. I just don't like being left out, as childish as it sounds."

"You need to know what's going on," Danil said easily, ushering the two of them to a seat each. "And we mental magicians sometimes need a kick in the pants to remember our manners. Speaking of magic, though, who taught you to shield so well?"

"Natural talent," Madam Seher said at the same time George waved a hand in her direction.

"Don't be silly, you did more than a little to help us hone the skill."

"Us?" Danil queried as he set lanes of bread on the table with a slab of butter.

"Both of my children seemed to inherit the same aptitude for shielding, and Seher made sure they were well prepared for… well, for what ended up happening, really." George grabbed a roll and started buttering it. "Adeline worked hard at it. Young George? Not so much."

"In all honesty, I thought it was a useless practice," Seher said quietly. "I had no idea there were so many magic users that could warp a mind like that. I thought I might even be the only one." Catching Danil's pause as she reached for a roll herself, she quickly clarified. "Oh, I only use the magic for my shows and to break up a few fights every now and then. Never would have occurred to me to use it for ill gain."

"We suffered the same blindness," Danil said. "Rogan trained at the Temple under the same man that taught Julianne. All we teach is kindness and empathy. I have no idea how he warped that into such a horrible thing."

"I do," Julianne said as she stepped inside and took off her robe. She hung it on the hook just inside the door. "Or, the little bit I do know is enough to make a guess. One of his cult members once heard him reference the Boulevard as home."

"Oh." Danil's eyes widened a little, and he explained for their guests. "The Boulevard is the slum quarter of Arcadia. Until recently, the penalty for someone there using magic was death."

"Death? For living with a blessing from Bethany Anne herself?" George asked, shocked.

"Who's dead?" Marcus stomped in, and stopped to wipe mud off his boots at the door. His boots were caked with it, though, and eventually, with an apologetic grimace, he gave up and slipped them off.

"Socks, too, you smelly man," Julianne admonished, then pointed at his feet. "Can you go wash those horrid things under a tap somewhere?"

"My toes will freeze off!" Marcus protested.

"Plenty of food to warm them back up again," Danil said with a grin. "And if you don't, I'll make sure you suffer the stink twice as bad as I do."

Grumbling, Marcus headed back outside and returned a few minutes later, feet dripping. Danil threw him a towel he had collected, and Marcus finally took his seat at the table as Danil brought out the food.

George watched the exchange with interest. He had heard so many rumors about the small group who had turned up in Tahn and proceeded to not only liberate the village, but stay on and help them rebuild.

He didn't ask the many questions he had; rather, he allowed the conversation to drift, first covering the recent revolution in Arcadia, which it seemed most of Julianne's friends had taken part in, and the history of his own city, Muir.

"So," George finished up, "the little village my grandfather helped to defend kept growing. The bigger we got, the better we could fight off those damned remnant, and the more civilized we became. By the time magic started appearing, my father was already grooming me to take his place as the leader of my people."

"So, you're not a *real* lord, then?" Marcus asked casually.

"Why?" George countered. "Are you planning to lead my people in a revolt against me?"

Marcus blushed and tried to offer an apology for the poorly-worded question, but George just laughed. "Only joking, my boy. I know you did a service to your people back in Arcadia, and it seems like you're set on doing the same in Muir—against Rogan. But, what will you do afterwards?"

Marcus shrugged, seeming unworried by his inability to answer. George, however, noted Julianne was paying very close attention to the young soldier's response.

"I guess I'll go home. See if these magician friends of mine need a hand in their tower. Surely, they need someone to muck out the latrines every now and then?" he shot Julianne a sideways glance, but she just raised her eyes to the ceiling and shook her head.

"Would you consider staying for the right offer?" George asked after a pause.

Marcus looked interested at that, and leaned closer. "What do you mean?"

"Tahn is growing, and I've clearly failed in my duty to protect it. You've got the population here to sustain the army you've set up—how would you feel about taking on the role of Captain?"

"I'd... have to think about it," Marcus stammered. The offer had clearly taken him by surprise. He and Julianne shared a tortured glance.

"Of course, any of your people are welcome to stay with you. You'll need to promote a first and second lieutenant, and choose a third person if you don't intend to stay on." George wiped his face with a napkin. "But if you do, the army is yours."

"It's a generous offer," Danil said politely. "Do you mind if I ask your plans for the rest of the town?"

"Well, if your young apprentice is to have his way, I'll need to make some!" George noted the confusion on Danil and Julianne's faces. "Bastian told me about his idea for a school of magic, though he stressed he needed approval from his own leaders first."

"He doesn't, really," Julianne said, mind racing with the possibilities. She had spoken to Bastian about his plans, and said she would do what she could to support them once Tahn was safe. She hadn't realized he had put this much thought into it, though.

"Nothing can be done until you're home safe," Danil pointed out.

His words cast a pall on the group as they came back down to reality. Long term dreams were one thing, but for the immediate future, they had a fight on their hands. And George knew his next demand wouldn't go down favorably.

"We can't launch an attack until my daughter is safe," George said.

He was met with silence. Madam Seher glared at the others as if daring them to object. Marcus's face fell, as he realized the implications, and Danil winced in commiseration with his friend.

"He's right," Julianne finally said, heaving a sigh.

"I am?" George asked in shock.

"He is?" Danil echoed.

"Adeline is too valuable, both as a person and as an asset," Julianne explained. "If Rogan can exploit her as a hostage, he won't hesitate."

"Muir needs her," Madam Seher agreed.

"Then I guess we'll just have to go get her," Marcus said before looking around. "Where's dessert?"

CHAPTER SEVEN

Julianne maneuvered her way into the hall and cursed as a length of fabric caught her shoe and almost sent her tumbling. A sense of déjà vu passed over her, and she called out for Tansy.

"Didn't you say this pile of clothes was to be washed yesterday? Someone is going to break a leg in here."

"I washed it all. This is today's pile."

Deftly taking the tray off Julianne, Tansy held it aloft with one hand and made her way to the table. "Jakob! Food's here!" Her bellow echoed in the hall, bringing a crowd of people who snatched up plates and napkins on their way.

Marcus brought in a giant pot of boiled oats and Danil followed with two large jugs of milk. Behind them, Garrett pranced in holding a small bowl of brown sugar.

"Quit yer bellyachin', it wasn't that far!" the rearick teased.

"You're not the one lugging in half a field of wet oats," Marcus groaned. "How'd you get out of the hard work?"

"Me stubby legs weren't long enough, and that pot would have buried me in the dirt," he explained joyfully. "And me stubby wee hands couldn't hold the jugs. But mostly I was the only one Annie trusted with the most important part."

"Garrett, you're only six inches shorter than me," Marcus said.

"Well, maybe ye should remember that when yer puttin' shite on me for bein' short," Garrett shot back.

He carefully set the sugar on the table like it was a valuable jewel, then gave a bow. "At yer service, Miss Tansy."

Tansy bent down to kiss Garrett on the cheek, the action giving him a direct view down her tight top. "Pick your chin up off the floor, rearick," she snapped. "Or I'll tell your girlfriend."

"Me what? I don't have a girlfriend." He contemplated that a moment, then added, "Unless someone's been tellin' ye different. Have they?"

Tansy giggled at his hopeful look, and she shook her head. "Not a word. But if you want one, I'd suggest keeping your eyes to yourself."

"Aye, ye got a point, lass. And ye have my apologies if I offended ye."

"I make a living from men who want to look down my top, and I can't say I mind. Still, if you want to get anywhere with Bette…"

Garrett jumped. "What? Who said that? I didn't say that!"

"So... you *don't*?" Tansy teased.

"I didn't say that either!" Garret coughed and tugged at his collar, unsure how the hole he was in kept getting deeper. "I'm gonna go, now."

"Goodbye, Garrett!" Tansy waved cheerily before dissolving into stitches.

"Tansy, if you keep teasing him like that, he'll implode," Julianne admonished.

Tansy made a half-hearted attempt to control her giggles. "He makes it so easy, Julianne."

"I know." Julianne allowed herself a smile.

She as much as anyone wished that Garrett and Bette would hurry up and confess their feelings for each other. The two had danced around the issue since they had met, but Julianne wouldn't force the issue. They would have to come to it in their own time.

"So, what brings you down here to slum it with the kooks and the dancers, Jules?" Tansy asked casually.

Julianne was no fool. Tansy knew something was up. "I'm planning a short trip," she said in a low voice. "But I don't want word to get out."

"Oh?" Tansy leaned closer. "What's going on?"

"Hunting expedition," Julianne said, watching to see if Tansy would buy their cover story.

If the New Dawn found out about a rescue attempt, Julianne was sure Adeline wouldn't live to see the next day. They couldn't be sure a cult member wasn't lurking around outside the town, reading the minds of those they passed close enough to.

"Ah. You don't want a bunch of people tagging along?"

Julianne nodded, seeing Tansy had guessed the excuse she had ready if needed. "Exactly. We'll take a nature mage and see if they can rustle us up a few meals. I'll go in case we run into trouble. Do you think we could convince Jakob to come?"

"Come on, let's ask him." Tansy reached down to grab Julianne's hand and pull her up. "He's hiding over there in the corner."

As Julianne stood, she felt a spike of worry from Danil. She spotted Polly making an angry beeline for him.

Sorry, I have work to do. That one's all yours, she sent. Danil needed to work this out himself.

I hate you, Danil replied before pasting a fake smile onto his face to greet Polly.

The girl looked furious and Danil's smile faltered as she stormed up and poked a finger in his chest.

"Outside. Now," she demanded before storming off again.

As Danil hurried to catch up, he dipped into her mind and saw a memory of the night before. Polly had been heading over to apologise to him when she saw Julianne head inside. Staying in the shadows to wait until she had gone, Polly then saw the others arrive for their meeting.

She was no fool, and had immediately realized they were planning something important.

"Polly, we didn't leave you out intentionally. It was just import—"

"You *read* my *mind*?" she hissed, fury rising. "You filthy little scum sucker! I knew I couldn't trust you, but this really takes the cake!"

"I… ahh, shit. Polly, I didn't mean to." Danil rubbed his hands over his face, glad for the cool morning breeze that fanned his skin.

They were behind the barn at the back of the hall, probably to take advantage of the little bit of privacy the hidden corner offered. He wasn't about to read Polly's mind again to verify that theory, though.

"You didn't mean to disrespect my privacy? Abuse the power you have over everyone else? The people of Tahn look up to you, Danil, and I'm struggling to understand why."

Her words hit him like a slap in the face. "Polly, I'm sorry. Really, truly sorry. The villagers here know why I'm in their heads, and none of them have said a word about it. I've spent so long living in the Mystic Temple, dipping in and out of people's heads, that sometimes I just forget it's not polite."

She opened her mouth again, but he cut her off gently. "I know that's not an excuse. I really am sorry, though, and I promise I won't do it again without permission."

Polly paused, then grumbled, "Fine."

Now completely out of her head, and with no one around to let him use their eyes, Danil stood in darkness. If he tried, he would be able to see what was happening in the hall—but that would just disorient him. Instead, he waited patiently for Polly to speak.

"I know you think I'm nothing, Danil, but that's just because I *have* nothing here." It was her turn to ignore his protest. "Let me speak. I know whatever you spoke to Seher and George about was important and probably a secret, but at least the theatre troupe has someone to speak on their behalf. I don't."

"I… hadn't thought of it that way," Danil admitted.

"Seher leads her people. I lead mine. All three of them," she added, referring to the girls who had fled the brothel with her. "And even though you think I'm just some nuisance tagging along, I have a responsibility to those women, and a right to decide what to do myself. I can't do that if I don't know what's going on."

Surprised at her reasoned argument, Danil nodded. "Ok. But I still can't tell you what's going on. You can't shield, so if we've been infiltrated—which is a possibility—you might not be able to keep our secrets."

"So, your answer to that was to leave me in the dark completely?"

Danil sighed. "Polly, I don't have any more experience dealing with any of this than you do. I'm not a leader, or an organizer, or even a *damned* teacher, no matter what people think. I'm making my own way in the dark, too."

He gave a wry chuckle at his own words, reflecting how dark it really was when he didn't have someone else's sight to rely on.

"Bullshit," Polly said. "You can't even look me in the eye when you say it."

Embarrassed, Danil adjusted his gaze to where he thought she was. "Is this better?"

"You're a dick."

"Hey, you're the one who wanted me out of your head. Do you see anyone else around I can use for eyes?" he snapped. This girl was really getting under his skin.

"What are you *talking* about?" Polly said. "Use your own damn eyes."

"Oh." Danil's irritation faded. "You don't know, do you? I'm blind."

"A blind fool," Polly muttered. Then, seeing he was serious, she gasped. "Oh. Great, now I look like an asshole, don't I?"

"Not at all. How were you supposed to know?" Danil offered a reassuring smile. "I pride myself on hiding it, for the most part."

Polly sighed. "You use other people's eyes to see, don't you?" she guessed. "That's why your magic is always on."

Danil nodded. "For the most part, I can 'borrow' someone's vision without touching their thoughts. If that person is really emotional, though, sometimes stuff kind of leaks out."

"That's why you read my mind."

Warm skin touched Danil's arm as the wall beside him thudded gently. He turned his head, guessing she was beside him. "Like I said, no excuse. I knew you were angry about something when you walked up to me; I should have shielded myself off better."

Silence fell over them, buffered by the sound of two people breathing in the warm morning sun.

Eventually, Danil spoke. "Polly, I don't know why I keep fighting with you. You're smart, and strong, and you're doing your best to look after your people."

More silence. Then, Polly moved away. "Can we just start again?" she asked.

"Sure," Danil said easily.

A hand took his and shook it firmly. "Hi. I'm Polly. Polly the prostitute."

Danil chuckled. "And I'm Danil, the blind fool. Pleased to meet you, Polly."

CHAPTER EIGHT

Adeline sat by her window, looking out. The sun beat on the dirty glass, making her skin damp with sweat. Below, the streets were quiet.

She jumped up when someone knocked at her door. She quickly buttoned her dress to her throat, deciding the stifling heat in the room was worth putting up with to hide every bit of skin possible from that lecherous mental mage.

"Come in," she called.

To her surprise, the man that entered was tall and young.

"You're not my father," she said, noting the irony—it was *never* her father coming through that door. Just a slimy imposter.

"Ah, of course. You wouldn't remember me." The man picked up a seat by her dresser and brought it over to her. "My name is Rogan."

She didn't bother to fake surprise. "Of course, you are." Adeline bit the inside of her mouth, then smiled to soften her words. "My father has told me so much about you."

"Such spirit." His eyes locked on hers, refusing to let go. "I thought we might dine together tonight. You could get to know me beyond what your... *father* has said."

Adeline angled a glare at him. This man had taken her city from her, had run her father out of town. She didn't want to dine with him. She wanted to stab him in the throat.

She reached a hand out to touch his, a tiny smile pulling at her mouth as he sucked in a sharp breath. "That sounds wonderful. Will you be joining me in my room?" She hadn't left this blasted cage in weeks, except to visit the tower to send her messages to Seher.

"Oh, no. The staff have prepared a feast in the dining hall." Rogan sounded out of breath and his cheeks flushed pink.

Bile rose as Adeline realized she'd practically propositioned him with her poor choice of words. Still, she could work it to her advantage.

Adeline drew her hand away, allowing one finger to trail across his wrist. "I do hope you'll ask them to bring out the good wine."

Rogan grinned, chin trembling slightly. "Of course. I'll do that now. You should come down as soon as you're dressed."

He stood and walked quickly to the door, sparing her only the shortest of glances as he left. He looked as if he'd been kissed by the moon.

Adeline flew to her feet, yanking out dress after dress and tossing them on her bed. She picked up one, a brilliant red gown with a startlingly white lace veil. She'd had it made for a masquerade ball, but didn't think Rogan would know it was a style not usually worn by local women.

Madam Seher's seamstress had made it, and hidden pockets deep in the skirt for bags of sparkling dust to fling at the ball.

The pockets were perfect to slip a thin dagger in one and a heavy crystal stone in the other. Neither were designed as weapons. The dagger was blunt from the thousands of letters she'd opened with it, and the crystal was a pretty decoration that just happened to have a few jagged edges and some weight to it.

It would have to do. She wasn't planning on killing Rogan

tonight, anyway. She needed more information first. Who was working for him, where, and what would happen to the spells he had cast on them if he died.

Tonight was reconnaissance, and she would do anything it took to get that information out of him. As she touched some pink powder to her face, she smiled. Finally, she was fighting back.

CHAPTER NINE

They met outside the walls of Tahn. Julianne, with Marcus at her side as always, arrived just after sunset. Jakob, the physical mage, and Mathias, Seher's nature magician, were already waiting for them.

The two made a contrasting pair, Jakob with his close-cropped, jet-black hair and overgrown muscles, Mathias weed-thin with long, blonde hair pulled off his face with a leather cord. Their personalities were so similar, though, they could have been brothers.

Both had a deep appreciation for humor and hearts soaked with honor. They had ridden ahead of their theatre troupe when Tahn was under attack, lending their magic and their fists to the battle.

They had also drunk their fair share of the victory mead afterwards.

Marcus eyed their horses appraisingly. "Nice," he commented. "I don't remember seeing them in town."

"They're wild," Mathias explained.

Marcus stepped back as one of the horses bared its teeth and huffed at him. "Ah. Seher said you'd provide a horse for Adeline?"

Mathias grinned, his white teeth sparkling in the moonlight. "Jakob's mount is sturdy enough for two."

"Can't argue with that." Mounting his own horse, Marcus looked back at Julianne. She was staring at Mathias, eyes narrowed. "You ready, Jules?"

Snapping out of her deep thoughts, she climbed onto Cloud Dancer and gave the horse a pat. She seemed almost glad to see the gentle mare again—surprising, because as a rule Julianne didn't like horses.

"Let's go." Marcus nudged his horse and left the way out of town, though soon dropped back to speak to Julianne.

Her attention, however, was on Mathias. "Show me your ears," she said unexpectedly.

"Jules, why in the world—Oh!" Marcus jumped when the nature magician obliged, pulling his hair back to display sharply pointed ears. "You're a druid?"

"Catches on quick, this one," Mathias said with a chuckle.

"What are you doing out this way?" Julianne asked.

"I took my *Versuch* because I couldn't stand being cloistered in that jungle," he admitted. "Getting out was like a breath of fresh air, and travelling with the theatre? Every day is like a sip of fine wine after a lifetime of drinking sour milk. Though I loved my family and even the Forest, that life just isn't for everyone."

"I can relate to that," Julianne said with a small smile. She glanced at Marcus, the look of wistfulness almost hidden by the deep shadows of the forest.

"Do you have news of my people?" Mathias asked eventually. He sounded almost reluctant to hear the answer.

"They seem to be surviving, as they always have," Julianne said. "Did you hear about the trouble in Arcadia?"

"Somewhat. Adrien finally showed his true colors?"

"If by 'true colors' you mean 'shade of asshole', then yeah," Marcus answered. "Ran the place with an iron fist that came down on the poor all too often."

Mathias nodded. "And some girl ousted him. Did my people help?"

Julianne and Marcus exchanged glances. Initially, the druids had refused to help. "Laurel came," Julianne said.

Mathias raised an eyebrow. "She was just a child when I left. An obstinate, pig-headed, troublemaker, but a child nonetheless." A soft smile touched his lips. "Yes, if any were to break away and help lead a revolution, it would be Laurel."

A lapse in conversation brought a question to Marcus's mind. "Mathias, if you can heal, why is George still limping?"

"That bastard Rogan didn't choose his words carefully enough. When he told his goons to 'throw him in a cell', they literally threw Lord George into a wall. He broke his ankle when he fell, and it had already started to set wrong when I got to it."

"Damn," Marcus muttered, thinking of the gentle old man left in a dungeon with a broken foot.

"That man will have a reckoning the likes of which has never been seen," Mathias said quietly.

Marcus threw him an alarmed look. "We're here for Adeline, Mathias. Not war. Not yet."

Mathias's face broke into a sunny smile. "I'm a druid, friend. I have the patience of an ancient forest."

Marcus gave him an uneasy grin back, unsettled by the man's sudden mood changes. When Mathias dropped back to speak with Jakob, he sighed with relief.

"Are you sure you trust these guys?" Marcus asked.

"Their goals are aligned with ours," Julianne said cryptically. When Marcus gave a skeptical grumble in response, she added, "Yes. I trust Madam Seher, and I trust her people. I also—"

Julianne jerked her reins up and flicked one hand into the air, signaling them to halt. The sound of thundering hooves clattered down the road, the noise echoing in the night air.

Four soldiers wearing the colors of George the Third's

personal army came galloping towards them. Julianne yanked out her staff.

These men had murder in their eyes, but their minds were broken with fear and grief. A seed of pity warred against the instinct for self-preservation.

"Try not to kill them," Julianne called to the others.

One of the horses peeled off and ran back the way it came. Its rider screamed and kicked it, jerking the reins, only to be thrown off before the horse fled into the night.

Mathias grinned, his eyes flashing green. "One down. Don't hurt the animals, please."

Marcus lifted his magitech rifle and let off a round just as the two parties met. He closed his eyes to protect them from the flash of light as he fired into a soldier, knocking him off his horse.

The two remaining fighters slammed into Marcus, perhaps because he looked the most dangerous—but looks could be deceiving.

As Marcus lifted his temporarily useless weapon to block a sword swing, he saw Jakob's hands move. One of the soldiers was jerked from his horse onto the ground.

The other ducked a jab from Marcus only to crumple to the ground as Julianne's staff smashed him in the side of the head.

"Thanks," Marcus panted, but mustered up a grin for her.

Jakob lifted a hand and a glowing flame jumped up from his palm, lighting the ground. Marcus looked around. The soldier he had blasted was lying still on the ground. The one whose horse had bolted was gone.

"Dammit." Jakob spat at the ground. "One got away." He regarded the other two, one unconscious, the other struggling against invisible bands around his body.

Marcus slid off his horse and thumped the wriggling soldier in the head. His eyes rolled back, and he stopped moving.

"Marcus!" Julianne chided. "I wasn't finished!" Her eyes cleared enough to glare at him.

Marcus winced. "Sorry. Did you get anything from him?"

"Enough," she said, sighing. "The remains of the army is still together, barely. They're following George—the younger one—but he's out of his mind. They all need a good feed and a warm bed, but they refuse to leave him, and he won't go back to Muir."

"Do they pose a danger to Tahn?" Jakob asked. "If so, we should go back to warn them."

Julianne shook her head. "There are less than two dozen men left. Bette will handle them if they get too close."

Marcus winced again—this time, thinking of the pain those men would feel if they tried to attack Tahn while Bette was manning the defenses.

CHAPTER TEN

Adeline took a sip of wine, looking over the glass at Rogan through her long eyelashes. She had darkened them with a little powder tonight, and used cream to gloss her lips to a pretty shine.

It seemed to have worked. When she had descended the stairs from her room, Rogan's eyes had almost fallen out of his head. The form-fitting gown was tighter than when the dress was made, and her breasts threatened to spill over the top.

Adeline had thrown the veil away, but her pockets hid more than one weapon. Now, watching him, she struggled to keep her eyes on him and not drop to the knife.

"And the insolent witch cast illusions, mirroring herself into a hundred images. My soldiers didn't know where to look, who to attack. One even hit his own friend in the nose, can you believe it?"

Rogan giggled gleefully, as proud of Julianne's magic as if he himself had pulled off the trick that had confused them so badly.

"And then what happened?" Adeline asked, hand to her throat as she mimicked concern.

"I saw through it, of course." Rogan's grin dropped to a sly smirk. "I took a knife and drove it straight through her heart. Rebels and insurgents will never find a way to the throne while I'm in charge."

He watched her closely for a reaction. Adeline clapped. "Oh, how clever." She took another sip of wine to cover her seething irritation.

My father doesn't sit on a throne, you pompous asshole, she thought. *And when Julianne comes back, she'll hold you down while we take turns kicking your ass.*

Setting her glass down carefully, she met his eyes. "But, Rogan... what if Julianne had hurt you?" She forced her eyes wide open in a show of fear. "What if... what if she'd *killed* you?"

Rogan tentatively reached out and placed a hand on hers. "The loss would pain you, I know. But rest assured, my grand plans would still play on, and my death would be swiftly avenged." Rogan's dark eyes sparkled with delight, making Adeline shiver.

She swallowed the hard lump in her throat. "But how, Rogan? How will you—*we*—ensure that happens?"

He fell silent, chewing a mouthful of beef as he thought. Adeline turned her hand over underneath his, so she was holding his hand. Rogan sucked in a breath.

I can't believe he's so arrogant, he's falling for this, she thought as she gave him a sweet smile. *As if any woman could care for a whimpering lentil like Rogan.*

Adeline withdrew her hand. "I'm sorry. I shouldn't pry. After all, you have no reason to trust me." She slipped her hand under the table to hide it as she wiped it on her skirt. *Ugh. He's sweaty, too.*

Rogan opened his mouth to speak. She pretended not to see it and cut him off. "This food is delicious. Margaret, could you fetch the chef so I can give him my thanks?"

Margaret, the serving girl, dipped a curtsey. "Of course, Ma'am."

"Wait!" Rogan hastily wiped his mouth. "No need to bother him. Let us take a walk in the gardens, my dear, so I can answer your questions. You *do* have my absolute trust, of course, you do."

Adeline nodded to Margaret. The girl skittered over to take the napkin from Adeline's lap, then began to clear the table, shooting worried glances at her mistress. Adeline ached to give her a sign, some small reassurance that it was all an act and she hadn't fallen under Rogan's spell.

She didn't dare to. If Rogan used his mind-reading spell on Margaret, he would know something was amiss. Adeline had to see this through, she *had* to know what safeguards he had in place. Otherwise, she could set off a catastrophe when she killed him.

"Why do you want to know about my plans, Adeline?" Rogan didn't sound upset, but his moods could change on a whim.

Adeline debated pressing him hard, but decided against it. "I haven't had a chance to know you well, Master Rogan," She said, using the honorific he had bestowed on himself. "I only know that you were—are close to my father."

She silently cursed, hoping he hadn't noticed the slip. She wasn't supposed to know her father had gone missing.

"He has such excellent judge of character that I must believe you are an honorable man, worthy of my… attention." She casually caressed his arm, gratified to feel him shiver.

"Ah, of course. You are not particularly close to your father, though, are you?" Rogan asked as they stepped onto the gravel path leading to the gardens.

"Oh, I love him dearly," Adeline gushed, "even though he could be so stubborn. A girl has to have her fun, you know. If you don't let a bird out of her cage, how is she to learn how to fly?"

The reputation she had formed over the last few months was one of a hot-headed socialite. There was, in her opinion, no better way to lead a man to underestimate a woman than by letting them indulge their assumptions. She let the men around her believe she was flighty and stupid, and they never questioned it.

"A father's job is to smother his children." Rogan's voice drifted off and his steps slowed. "To pour love and attention on them, and coddle them in cotton wrap to keep them safe from imaginary danger."

Rogan reached a hand out to pluck a flower from a bush. Adeline prepared to take it from him… but he crushed it in his hand and tossed it on the ground.

"Sadly, not all fathers seem to understand that." He stepped around the corner.

"But, I digress." Rogan's voice softened and he turned a smile on for her, bright, yet brittle. "You seek a husband?"

Ice ran down Adeline's spine. "Why, yes, I'm of an age where it's becoming something of a necessity." She pouted her lips, looking up at him coyly. "I'll be old before you know it, and no man will want me." She *had* to get this conversation back on track.

"Oh, my beautiful, precious child." Rogan cupped her cheek and turned her face to him. "You are a stunning, delicate flower just beginning to bloom. Why, I should marry you myself if it weren't for…" he trailed off, but looked at her expectantly.

Fine, she thought. *I'll play.* "For what, dear Rogan?"

"Well," he started, then sank into himself. "I didn't think you'd want me."

The pitiful look on his face was so much like a child in the village who had lost a candy that Adeline teetered between scorn and repulsion. She had to take a steadying breath before she spoke again.

"I certainly don't wish to marry the insipid little boys I've courted so far. I need a man, Rogan, a strong man who can keep me safe, who can help Father and me build our city and make it strong."

Dammit, girl, just tell him you love him. Adeline couldn't do it, not even to save her own life. In fact, he could rip her toenails out and shove them in her eyeballs, and she still wouldn't say that to him.

She made do with batting her eyelids a few times. Even only that made him melt. "Oh, Adeline, the plans I have! I will make Muir an oasis, a refuge where people can be free of greed and envy, will work hard for the satisfaction of working. No one will steal, or lie, or cheat. They will all come together for the greater good to provide for all!"

He looked to the sky, the stars overhead reflected in his eyes. "Adeline, help me. Help me make this city of yours into paradise."

She stayed silent for a little while, and they walked on, feet scraping the loose stones on the rough path as they brushed past the pointed leaves of exotic plants her father had found.

"People don't like change, Rogan. What if they fight back? What if more like that—that Julianne girl come?"

The reminder of the rival mystic made his face twist in displeasure. "Then I will crush them, one by one," he whispered. "I will destroy them, if it's the last thing I do."

"And what of me, if your enemies come back? What will they do to me if I'm left alone and helpless?" Adeline asked breathily. She put a hand on his arm, her heart beating so hard with an anxious need to know his plan that she didn't have to fake her fear.

"They will lose everything," Rogan said, sneering. "If my personal guard see me die, they will be compelled to avenge my death even if it means their own. It *will* mean their own."

"What do you mean?"

"They will throw themselves off parapets and slit their own throats in mourning. The entire city will crumble, and those who rose against me will stand in broken streets, blood lapping at their boots, and know the price was never going to be worth the sacrifice they demanded." Rogan's chest heaved and panted as he ran out of steam.

"And me?" Adeline asked coolly.

"My dear Adeline." He pulled her into a hug. "Why would you ever want to live in a world without me in it?"

CHAPTER ELEVEN

Garrett heard Bette grumbling at the door as she jerked off her boots. Muttering a curse to himself, he dumped his own shoes through the barn window.

They had made a reasonable living space out of the old building. A wall was extended to the ceiling for privacy, and inside was freshly painted to neaten it up and cover the last of the stale horse smell.

The packed dirt floor was just like home, and indeed, Garrett had visions of himself as a teenager, sneaking out of his room to visit the fights or meet a pretty lass without his parents' consent.

He hoisted himself up and over the windowsill, cowering beneath the opening as Bette called out.

"Where are ye, ye stinking wee man? I know yer avoidin' me!"

He scrambled around the corner, cutting across the yard and hoping the long shadows of dusk was enough to cover his retreat. He didn't breathe again until the old barn was out of sight.

Slowing to a walk, Garrett began to whistle a tune. It wasn't that he was *afraid* of Bette, he reassured himself. He just didn't want to talk to her until he knew exactly what to say.

"Aye, I'll come up with somethin' tomorrow," he said to himself.

"Come up with what, rearick?"

Garrett jumped and spun, then put a hand to his thumping chest. "Mack, ye prick. Ye damn scared me half ta death!"

"Good!" Mack exclaimed, draping an arm over his short friend's shoulder. "Wouldn't want you to turn up for training without a strong heartbeat and a healthy sense of danger."

"Sod off, ye bastard," Garrett grumbled.

"You've been a right prick lately," Mack commented happily. "What's up your ass?"

Garrett scowled, unwilling to admit he had been losing sleep over a lass. "Ye think I'd tell ye after that?"

Mack shrugged. "You either need a fight or a fuck. Not much of either round here lately." The battle against Lord George's son had been just what the town needed to restore their confidence. Their losses had been low and their success swift.

The only downside was that it left most of the fighters wanting more. They knew—or they *thought* they knew—what battle was like, and they wanted to do it again.

"Enjoy the peace while it lasts, lad," Garrett said. "When a real war hits, the food goes ta shit and the price of a good fuck goes through the roof."

"Well, I never said I wanted war," Mack said, rapidly backtracking as he realized hot meals and pretty women might be at risk. "Just a good, old-fashioned dust up."

"Just keep yer nose clean and worry about yer trainin'," Garrett insisted.

When they reached the barracks, which was really just a small, wooden building at the front of the town, Mack slipped into place and obeyed Garrett's instructions. The evening class was the rearick's favorite—there was something invigorating about training by lantern light.

Not only that, it was the session most likely to include some of Madam Seher's theatre troupe. Every night, one or two performers at a time would wander in and take part in the grueling, repetitive drills.

They were never on time and rarely stayed the whole period, usually chased off by Garrett or Bette for disrupting their soldiers with funny tricks and lightning-fast moves.

Mack slipped into the various battle stances Garrett shouted out, then lined up on command for a sparring session. They had progressed from stabbing at bags of wheat and chaff to fighting each other, using blunt spears and wooden shields, crafted by some of the older folk in the village.

Mack faced off against his opponent, a slip of a figure hidden behind a tall, vertical shield. He waited for the command to begin.

"Go!" Garrett barked.

Mack took a few steps back to give himself room, but his sparring partner quickly stepped closer. Mack stopped, then slammed his smaller, round shield forwards against the other.

The other person stumbled back. Then, with a clatter and a slight *whoosh* of air, she tossed her own shield aside, darted towards Mack and jumped at his, launching into a flip as she sailed over his head.

"Dammit, Tansy," he complained when she landed with a satisfied smirk. "That's not fair, and you know it!"

"Just keeping you on your toes, beautiful."

Mack blushed at the compliment. He tapped an imaginary hat and bowed, then yelped as she cracked him on the head with a stick.

"Don't take those pretty eyes off your enemy!" she scolded.

"Aye. She's right," Garrett said, sauntering up. "You let yerself be distracted by a pretty face and ye'll get yer ass handed to ye on a platter."

"Is that why Bette's always kicking *your* ass?" Jarv called out.

Garrett flushed an angry red and rounded on him. "She could

kick the arse of any man she bloody well wanted. And if I hear one of ye, just *ONE* of ye claimin' she only beat a man because he was distracted, I'll put ye in a match against her meself. Hear me?"

Jarv wiped the smile off his face and saluted. "Understood, Sir!"

The sniggers behind him were stifled enough that Garrett could ignore them. "Back to work ye bastards. Ten more minutes, and once yer asses are properly kicked, ya can go stand on the wall for an hour."

Groans and sighs met his words. The evening shift mostly comprised of the men who worked the fields during the day— they were already tired and an extra hour of standing around with nothing to do was *not* how they wanted to spend their evening.

"If ye do it right, there'll be a hot feed at the end of it." Garrett hoped he could follow through on that promise.

It worked. The soldiers brightened and went back to their training with gusto, the sound of wood against wood clacking through the night air.

Tansy left Mack to find another sparring partner. As she sauntered away, Garrett snagged her with a gesture.

"Do ye think ye could rustle us up some food? The old couple on the corner back there usually cook fer the men, but it might be a wee bit late."

"Sure, rearick," Tansy said. "We've got a pot of goat stew on at the hall, and I can pinch a bit of that if I can't find anything else."

"Thank ye, lass." He waved her off, glad that she and her friends were keeping his men on their toes. Since the fight against George's men, they had become just a little too confident for his liking.

"Garrett! Where's Garrett?" Sharne came pushing through the lines of sparring men, barely pausing to let them pull back fists and weapons.

"Over here!" He hurried over. Sharne was rostered on for wall duty—she wouldn't have left unless something had happened.

"Garrett, someone is camping out in the woods." Sharne leaned on her knees, panting.

"Eh?" Garrett squinted at her in confusion. Then, remembering Julianne's cover story, he stammered, "Ahh, that'll be the, err…"

"We're not idiots, Garrett." She gave him a withering glare. "We know Julianne took some people on a mission to Muir."

"Who the bloody hell told ye that?" he snapped.

"No one ratted them out, but you don't send a damn mystic leader and the head guardsman on a hunting party," she said flatly.

Garrett kicked the ground. Then, with a sniff, he pinned her down with a glare of his own. "Well, what of it? They're off doin' whatever they're doin'. What's goin' on in the woods, then?"

"We can smell roasting meat. The wind tonight is a southerly, so it's coming from that way." She pointed. "If Julianne is headed to Muir, she'd be that way." Sharne shifted her index finger over. "Plus, they only left at sundown. They wouldn't stop to eat an hour after leaving."

"Aye, yer right. Take two men; go scout it out."

Sharne saluted. "Permission to request an animal-speaker from Madam Seher?" she asked briskly.

Garrett narrowed his eyes warily. "Ye keep havin' ideas like that, ye'll be takin' me job. Aye, ask the old woman for one of her people."

Sharne took off at a run. Garrett rubbed his head, wondering if his hair really was thinning or if he was just paranoid. "Too fuckin' young ta be going bald, ye bastard," he muttered to himself. Then, louder, "Alright ye mangy pricks, get yer asses to the wall. Double-shift fer the next two days, and don't shoot yer squad leader when she goes out, *or* when she comes back."

<h1 style="text-align:center">CHAPTER TWELVE</h1>

Lawson paced around the sputtering fire, trying to ignore the aroma of fresh-cooked rabbit over a spit. There were only three—hardly enough for the dozen men that watched it roast, practically drooling on their boots.

"First one to our lord," he snapped as one of the men stood to pull them off the fire.

Any grumbles of discontent were quickly smothered. They were the last of their army, loyal to a fault and willing to follow their lord into any battle... or, in this case, in random circles around the countryside.

During the battle of Tahn, Lord George the Third had suffered some kind of injury. Perhaps it was some kind of "Bastard-spawned magic," as the men had claimed. Lawson suspected it was more likely a knock to the head.

It was irrelevant. They had pledged their lives to their leader, and would follow him to the grave.

Still, there were opportunities to be had. Twice, they had found old farms outside the village proper as they circled around Tahn at their master's command. Their raids had uncovered a few crocks of preserved vegetables, and potatoes buried deep enough that they were still edible, though a little green.

He knew if they could get into the town, they could empty a few cellars and eat well for days.

"Arnold," Lawson called and beckoned his second over to talk.

"You still on that hare-brained plan of yours?" Arnold asked. He darted a glance back at George. Their lord was chewing slowly as one of the men fed him strips of meat. The soldier jerked his hand as George bit hard on a fingertip.

Lawson ignored the look of disgust on Arnold's face. "We're close enough to town. You and me can go in and have a look around. They don't know we're here."

"Oh, they don't, do they? What about that witch and her friends that killed Wallace?"

Four soldiers had encountered a woman from Tahn, the one rumored to have caused George's condition. Only three had eventually returned. "I sent Antony to examine their tracks. They were headed to Muir, and unless they flew back, they didn't return."

Arnold frowned and looked away. Lawson set his jaw, staring the man down, daring him to argue.

"Yes, Sergeant. What are your orders?"

"Wait until the men are asleep. I don't want anyone thinking they'll sneak along behind us for a free feed. Tell the watch you're going for a piss, and wait for me behind that gully over there." Lawson jerked his head towards a dried-up creek. "Moon should be gone by then."

Indeed, a heavy cloud bank was slowly moving in from the east. Arnold shivered as a chill breeze brushed past. "Right." He stomped off and tucked himself into his bedroll. A few jeering calls were sent his way, but he warded them off with a surly look.

Lawson's eyes fell on his lord for a moment. George's greasy chin shone in the firelight, ignored as the young lord sat cackling to himself about nothing. Lawson simply turned his back on the sweaty, uncouth soldiers. Staring out into the night, he vowed he would take revenge for what the people of Tahn had done to his army.

To anyone watching, he would have looked like a statue carved from stone. No one was, though. Lawson knew the watch were slacking, discipline once worn with pride now discarded in the face of this minor difficulty. When the hour grew late and their meagre rations had been depleted even more, the men eventually rolled into tents and began to snore.

The watch patrol—a mere three men—idled nearby, talking. Not one of them saw their sergeant standing off to the side, nor did they notice when he quietly walked away.

One of the watch gave Arnold a wave, but no one bothered to ask where he was going. He had his excuse ready—and in fact, he was dying for a piss, having held on so he didn't raise questions by going out a second time.

Wouldn't have bloody mattered, he thought to himself as he sprayed the bushes. *Those morons wouldn't notice a herd of wild hogs sitting by the fire and eating our dinner.*

He took a minute to savor the feeling of a now-empty bladder, then set off to meet Lawson.

"Took your bloody time," the sergeant muttered.

"Sorry, Sir," Arnold said. He didn't bother offering an excuse—his sergeant had told him to wait until the others were asleep, and he had. Lawson was an asshole, though, and Arnold knew better than to argue.

Without saying anything else, Lawson took off, his long, powerful strides through the densely wooded forest seeming effortless to Arnold, whose short legs struggled to keep up.

The trees ended a short trek from Tahn. The distant glow of light rose above above the crooked wall that had been damaged during the battle and apparently not yet repaired.

Arnold risked a few words. "Where are we entering, Sir?"

Lawson briskly gestured for him to be quiet and Arnold

winced. He would be punished for that later, he was sure. So, he shut his mouth, kept his head down, and followed his sergeant along the tree line once the lights had dwindled.

The two men cut across a field as the moon dipped behind a cloud, sticky mud sucking at their boots as they raced with the shadows. The easy run they had expected took far longer than Lawson had anticipated, due to a murky bog hiding beneath the lush grass.

Reaching the wall, they tumbled against it, panting after an exertion they had grown unused to in the previous weeks.

Lawson made a hand gesture, signaling Arnold to follow the wall along to the east. Lawson kept on his tail, smirking when the smooth, white wall suddenly changed to rough-hewn timber. A short distance from there, it stopped.

Lawson guessed the villagers either thought they were far enough from the town's entrance that it didn't matter, or, more likely, they had simply run out of materials. Or, perhaps, they had relied on the thick bog to slow any advancing army.

They slipped through a simple wooden fence designed to keep livestock in, but did little to keep the two men out. A horse in the corner of the field snorted and stamped his feet, but otherwise ignored them.

"Split up," Lawson whispered into Arnold's ear, making him jump. "Meet back at camp."

He knew Arnold was at least smart enough not to lead anyone back to their campsite, though he was tempted to give a stern warning anyway. He bit the words back and moved along the fence line, watching his soldier head for a small barn on the property.

He debated following him. Arnold was soft, a man who cared too much about the weak and desperate. Lawson knew his subordinate would have preferred to serve in the Muir army rather than with young George, and he despised that lack of integrity.

To Lawson, a person gave everything to the place they were assigned to, no matter their personal preference.

Lawson wandered, unhurried, looking for what he needed. He found a road and walked along it for a short distance, then veered off into another field. A house lay beyond it, and his eyes were drawn to the flickering lantern hanging from the porch.

If the light was outside, then someone was expected home. Probably the man of the house, he guessed—no woman would be out that late at night. The inhabitants were likely women, maybe some children.

"Just ripe for the picking," he muttered with a grin. Maybe he would get the chance to feed more than one type of hunger tonight.

Lawson kept an eye out for movement, but saw none. The night was getting on, and the moon had slipped behind another cloud by the time he reached the little cottage. He crept up to the window and looked inside.

The house was dark and quiet. A floorboard creaked gently on the porch and he froze, waiting twenty heartbeats before easing off it gently. When he touched the door, it swung open noiselessly.

Sharne lay in her bed, breathing slowly. The scouting trip earlier that evening had taken longer than expected—she had watched the soldiers long enough to establish they weren't moving out anytime soon, then gone back to report to Bette and Garrett.

By the time she had gotten home, she had barely had the energy to kick off her boots and throw her spear in the corner. Except, now something had woken her from a deep, exhausted sleep.

It was the floorboard, the one her mother wanted fixed, but her father wouldn't touch. She knew this was why—so that anyone at home would be alerted if someone approached the house. Now, she waited.

Easing a short sword out from beneath her bed, she watched the dim gleam of light beneath her door stretch as the lamplight leaked inside. She gripped the weapon, feeling its comforting weight even as she wished for the spear across the room, the one she had trained with day after day until it felt like an extension of her arm.

Something bumped gently in the hall and boots scraped softly past her door. So, they were going straight for her mother's room. They would get a hell of a shock when they got there.

Sharne slipped out of bed, leaving the sword on her blanket. She picked up the spear as her bare feet flitted past, and she eased her door open.

Counting silently to three, she threw caution and quiet to the wind as she took three running steps. She saw the shadow in the doorway ahead move, turning back towards her.

Lawson spun too late. A thrust of the spear landed in soft flesh. He cried out and Sharne jerked the shaft back as the lamp in the room ahead flared.

She saw a soldier, his bulky silhouette turning. Another jab, this time at his neck, missed as he jerked back.

"Ma! Raise the alarm!" Sharne yelled. She barely had time to react as a fist headed for her face. She darted back into the narrow hall, and stabbed with the spear. This time, it found a home in the soldier's thigh.

The intruder yelled, then barreled forwards, taking her off-guard. He slammed into her, pushing her to the ground and driving a boot into her chest. Sharne gasped for air, her lungs stunned from the blow and refusing to cooperate.

She groaned and rolled over, forcing herself to her feet to give chase as finally, the ability to breathe crept back.

Lawson didn't bother to look back. He ran, bumping into walls as he ploughed down the narrow hallway and tripped into the doorframe. Doing his best to ignore the twin burning sensations in his thigh and bicep, he staggered out, clipping the porch lantern with his shoulder.

An idea grabbed him, and he yanked it off the thin wire, then tossed it into a bush towards the back of the house. Glass tinkled as it smashed and a glow blossomed as the oil caught fire, sending thin flames licking at the dry leaves.

He hurried off at a jog, grunting in pain each time his weight landed on the injured leg. The door behind him clattered as the girl who had attacked him slammed it open and started after him.

He picked up speed, grinning when he heard a cry of "Fire!" He risked a glance back—the girl had left off chasing him, running now towards the bright glow of the grass fire.

Lawson ran on, aiming for the field he had cut across earlier. He thanked the thick cloud bank and hoped beyond hope it wouldn't rain. He needed them distracted for as long as possible.

When he reached the wall, Arnold was nowhere in sight. Growling at his second's incompetence, he set off to return back to the campsite and his lord.

CHAPTER THIRTEEN

Donna stood in the hallway, listening to Rogan mutter to himself.

"The head is the key. The one who control the heads, control the snakes." He rambled on, talking about armies and cities and all the groups he wanted to conquer.

"Control the daughter; control her father." He stopped then, pausing to inhale a slow breath. "Ahh, Adeline. Beautiful, beautiful Adeline. So clever. So, so clever… not like the others. Stupid. Stupid, all of them."

His ranting slowed as he talked about his new crush, but his voice became fast and tight as he spat insult after insult.

Donna's face burned. She knew he was talking about her, about her failure. She hadn't brought Julianne to their side, nor had she killed her. Because of Donna, Julianne now posed a problem.

She leaned against the wall, biting her cheek. The taste of copper filled her mouth, but she didn't relax her jaw. The pain was the only thing she had left.

Since killing the two mystics back at the Temple, it had become easier to remember who she was. It brought her no peace. Instead, the image of Gunter's face stayed with her, his eyes wide with shock as she had sunk the knife into his chest.

He had started to whisper her name, but had died before he could finish.

She had spent the next days in a stupor. When her people had attacked Julianne's party on their way down from the Heights, Donna had watched on, unable to pull her fractured mind together enough to use magic any more complicated than a shield.

She had managed a semblance of her normal self, at least in front of the others. Rogan hadn't noticed her occasional lapses, moments where her brain drifted off to another place, a blink of time that, when she woke, might turn out to be minutes or hours.

In fact, Rogan hadn't noticed her much at all. *He's obsessed with that bitch,* Donna thought. *That vapid, attention-seeking whore isn't good enough for him. He deserves better, he deserves* me!

A part of her saw the disconnect: she was pining over the affection of a man she hated, who she desperately wanted to escape, while begging to spend her life by his side.

She pushed herself up, knees trembling, and took three steps down the hall, away from her master.

"Donna? Is that you?" Rogan called out, his vague, aimless mumbling interrupted.

"Yes," she said, frozen in place.

"Come here, my dear."

He hadn't called her that in weeks. Not since she had let Julianne escape from her grasp. Heart racing, she quickly turned and entered his throne room.

The old petitioning chamber Lord George had used was now Rogan's favorite place. He had set an ornately carved chair in the middle, and thick rugs delineated the room to form a clear boundary.

The thick, navy carpet surrounding his self-proclaimed 'throne' was his territory. The lowly townspeople and servants must stand on the ageing red. Only a select few might step off the red hall runner, onto Rogan's blue.

She hurried down the long, red path, stopping with the toes of her boots just shy of the end. She halted so abruptly, so close to stepping past it, that she almost tripped over herself.

Taking a step back to catch her balance, she bowed.

"My lord?" she asked, breathlessly.

Am I excited or afraid? she wondered. Her heart raced, and her feet still felt unsteady beneath her. *Does it matter?* She would do his bidding regardless.

"Donna, I'm so glad you were close. I need to know what the current status is of our army. I want to know how many men we have, how many horses, what food supplies would be needed for a one-week journey, and… everything else." He frowned, thinking.

"Everything, my lord?" Donna asked.

"Just tell me what we need to take the army to Tahn, and if we already have it or need to find it." Irritability leaked through his words. "I don't care if we have to take food from the poorhouse—just make it happen, and tell me if there is a shortfall."

"My lord, if I make it happen, there will be no shortfall." She'd been under his spell long enough to know how it worked. If he gave an order that couldn't be completed, a mind-slave could literally kill themselves trying.

"Wonderful," he replied with a smile. "I'm glad you understand."

Is he unaware of the danger, or does he not care? Donna hid a tiny smile to herself. *Well, at least he hasn't given me a deadline.*

As a mystic herself, she knew the trick was in the phrasing. A willing servant—or a stupid one—would take words at face value, adhering to the spirit of the instruction.

However, a subject forced to act against their better nature was harder to control. A smart one would figure out a loophole or clause where they could, to avoid doing what they were told.

She blinked. A face formed in her mind of a foot soldier Rogan had ensnared with his magic. Already angry at the world for no reason at all, Rogan had thrown a fit when a small bird had gotten caught in his room and shat on his bed.

"Catch it," Rogan had said. "Before it escapes."

The soldier hadn't had a chance. The high rafters and wide-open window allowed the bird an easy exit, and the soldier followed, caught under a compulsion that left him splattered on the stones below when he landed.

Donna remembered looking out the window and down to the stones below, wondering when it would be her turn to give her life to save her master's… or just to fulfill one of his many whims.

It didn't bother her. Rogan was her everything. She would die for him, even while fighting against it.

"Hey!" Rogan smacked her face, not hard, but enough to sting.

"Wha… sorry, my lord." She looked at the ground, wondering how he had gone from lounging in his chair to standing before her in the blink of an eye.

"Look at me," he ordered.

Her eyes met his, ice-blue to glowing white. She felt his presence brush against the shattered edges of her shield, the touch sending electricity down her spine.

"Hmm. I seem to have broken you, my dear." He placed his fingers on her temples and closed his eyes to concentrate.

Pain streaked through her mind as he poked and prodded, shoved and yanked.

"You have more holes in here than a block of good cheese!" He laughed at his own joke, though Donna was too tired to respond. "Oh. That was poor form, wasn't it? Doesn't matter, it's not like you care."

No, I don't, Donna thought. *But I'd like you to stop hurting me.*

Whether by chance or because he heard her thought, Rogan withdrew from her mind. Since the Temple, parts of her mind had been packed away behind a block of some sort—not a conscious shield, but hidden away where he wouldn't notice them.

It was the only way she had been able to hide her hate for Julianne, Adeline, and all the others he had given his attention to so freely.

She wished he would let her go, cut their bonds. She could be free. *I could wander the countryside or settle on a small farm. I could kill the mystic bitch, or your little lover, or even all of Muir. Or perhaps I'll find myself a husband and raise some goats for milk.*

Snapping back out of her reverie again, Donna realized Rogan had been talking the whole time.

"...the army will crush them, and she will be mine," Rogan said.

Donna nodded, not caring what he was talking about. Probably war on Tahn. He spoke of little else lately.

"And then, the old man will be dead, I will own both cities, and Adeline will be free to marry me." He threw himself back into the big chair. "What a wedding it will be, Donna. But we can't do it without you."

"Yes, my lord," she said, voice choked.

Seeing her distress, Rogan jumped up in a rare show of pity. One hand cupped her face. "Donna. Oh, poor, sweet Donna. I know how much you adore me, but don't you see? You can never be mine." He tapped her temple. "You're broken, dear, darling Donna."

"Yes," she croaked. "I'm broken. You need... someone better."

He cradled her in his arms and let her sniffle into his coat. His face by her ear, he whispered to her. "I will look after you, my pet. You will always have a place by my side. Just... don't make me discard you, like the others did."

A chill ran down her spine. *Discard?* she thought. *No, you killed them on a whim.*

She closed her eyes and inhaled his smell, wondering what she wanted most—to make him proud or to make him die.

CHAPTER FOURTEEN

Julianne called a halt once the sun had crept high enough that it sparkled through the dense forest trees. "We'll find an out of the way spot and rest up. I don't want us running into anyone who might take word back to Muir," she said.

Mathias sat, hands on his knees, and stared into the distance as his eyes turned green. A few minutes later, he stood and pointed. "There's a bit of an outcropping that way," he said. "It'll provide cover from the elements and hide us from the road."

They headed for camp, covering their tracks as they left the road and used fallen branches to disguise their makeshift shelter.

It wasn't long before Marcus and Julianne were stretched out side by side.

"Annie cooks a mean breakfast," Marcus said, rubbing his stomach. "Or do we call that dinner? I'm surprised you told her we were leaving, though."

Annie hadn't been there when they left, but a parcel wrapped in cloth was sitting by the door. It contained a loaf of bread, cheese, cold meats, and a little jar of hot bean mix that had been just as delicious eaten cold.

"I didn't." Julianne rolled over to face him. "Damned if I know how she does it, but she figured that one out on her own."

"Well, I'm not game to ask how," Marcus commented.

Jakob came to sit by them. "Mathias is sending his bird now. He said to come find him if you need another message sent back to Tahn."

"No," Julianne said. "They can manage on their own for now."

"You don't think we should tell them about the trouble we ran into?" Marcus asked.

Julianne shrugged. "You really think Garrett can't handle a dozen men? He's got Tahn locked down like like a virgin in a whorehouse and—"

Marcus sputtered a laugh. "You and whorehouses," he said. "Anyone would think you want to go work in one."

She shrugged. "Some of my best friends work in a whorehouse, thank you." Marcus stared, slack-jawed, and Julianne burst out laughing. "Ok, fine. 'An acquaintance' of mine works in one. Or, she did."

Dropping back onto his blanket, Marcus groaned. "That's it. I'm *never* going to the city with you again. Or even a mid-sized town. In fact, I'm taking you back to the Temple when this is done because I know damn well there are no prostitutes there to give you bad ideas."

"Are you sure about that?" Julianne asked, as innocently as she could manage. A moment later, she was laughing again. "Oh, Bitch take me. You are so much fun to tease," she whimpered as tears ran down her cheeks.

"I'm going to sleep," Marcus said grumpily.

"It's always the ones that complain the loudest that need a good mistress the most," Jakob mused.

"Stop making it worse, you brute." Marcus pulled his blanket over his head and turned his back on them.

Unable to prod him into any more reactions, Julianne eventually gave up. Rather than go straight to sleep, she drifted into a light, restorative mediation.

As her mind emptied, she stared at the soft, crinkled leaves on the ground by her face. Each edge was crisp, the veins showing clearly where the soft fibers of leaf had worn away with age.

She felt the vibration in the ground before she heard Mathias stomping back. He paused by her side, and through her connection with the world around her, she felt his eyes on her.

She rolled over and stood, motioning him away from the sleeping men.

"What is it?" she asked in a low voice.

Mathias handed her a small, rolled up bit of paper. She unrolled it and read the words scrawled in tiny print. *Do not kill Rogan. His magic will kill others when he dies.*

"A death spell," Julianne muttered. "There's more than one way around that, you cunning bastard."

Death spells had been studied in the Temple extensively, but only by the most trusted mystics there. A death spell cast by a mystic would trigger an action, feeling, or belief when the mystic died.

Most mystics knew of them, and even used them—a feeling of calm and peace that would unravel in loved ones when the mystic passed into the next realm, or in one pranksters case, three days of his friends bursting into cabaret songs at random intervals.

Selah had kept notes on more insidious applications, and how to counter them. In most cases, simply knowing in advance meant another mystic could bind the first spell and neutralize it.

Of course, the death spell would only be triggered if the target knew the mystic was dead. Hiding the death from the person affected could work, or at least buy time for counter measures. So could certain counter-spells, though they were harder to formulate.

"Shall we reply?" Mathias asked.

Julianne had discussed the initial message with him—that

rescue was coming, but lacking any details that may give them away.

She shook her head. "No. We continue as planned."

Mathias nodded and withdrew. Julianne watched as he disappeared into the trees. A moment later, a rustling in the leaves drew her eyes up overhead. Mathias had climbed into the branches and was now lying along one, draped comfortably despite being at least forty feet off the ground.

"Druids," Julianne said, shaking her head. "Strangest bunch of people I've ever met."

She returned to her own bedroll and settled back into her meditation.

CHAPTER FIFTEEN

Bette stretched her arms up, feeling her back lengthen with a satisfying crunch. By her calculation, it had been a good day and a half since she had seen a bed, and the cracks of sunlight splintering the dawn sky were an unwelcome reminder of that.

"And ye found nothin' else?" she asked Francis.

He shook his head. "Just the fight at Sharne's, and that one sighting of another man." He paused. "I know Gerard can be an idiot, but if he says he was sober, he meant it."

Gerard was the only person who claimed to have seen another man, and Bette still wasn't certain he hadn't just seen Sharne's attacker. Still…

"It'd be plain stupid for him to come alone. Makes sense there were two, and if Gerard saw one, well, he saw one." She poked her head outside and bellowed. "Garrett!"

"Aye, hold yer knickers, woman."

Bette tapped her foot impatiently. "How far away did ye say that wee army was?"

Garrett clicked his tongue. "On foot, a little under an hour?"

"For you?" she asked, "Or for someone whose ass is a little further from the ground?"

Garrett scowled. "Just because I'm not a clobberin' giant, doesn't mean I'm slow."

"Aren't all rearick your size?" Francis asked, genuinely curious. Looking now, he realized Bette was, indeed a good couple of inches taller than Garrett.

"All of ye, stop pokin' fun at me bloody height!" Garrett seethed. "Just because I'm short for me size, doesn't mean I can't kick both yer asses."

The fact that Bette had beaten him in more than one fight was irrelevant. This was his honor at stake.

Ignoring him, Bette turned to Francis. "Assume they could run here in half that. They came at sundown, so it's likely they'll come back under cover of night if they return. Ye think ye can extend that wall a little?"

"We're running out of building materials," Francis said. "I can try, but it likely won't be long enough to keep them out forever. If they're entering at the wall's end, though, they're cutting through bog. That will slow them down and wear them out."

He glanced at the nearby table and motioned for a bit of paper.

Bette handed it to him with a stump of charcoal.

"Here's the town," Francis said as he sketched, "and there's the wall. All this—" he shaded a section "—is marshland. It's knee deep in places and a few spots where you'll lose a whole cow."

He pointed to the army's location, then drew a line with his finger. "They'd save time going this way, even if it's longer. And if they try to go around the bog, they'll hit the mountains."

"So, if we post some sentries in this wee bit of open land here, and leave a few men up front, we'll head them off?" Garrett asked.

Francis nodded. "If they're dumb enough to cut through the marsh again, you'll be meeting them wet and tired. If they come to the front, the wall will slow them."

"Aye." Bette sighed. "Double shifts it is, then. Garrett, do ye think we should cancel training until the others get back?"

Looking surprised that she had asked him, he wrinkled his face, thinking. "Aye. We don't want ta run them inta the ground, and there's twice as much work ta do with that lot from Muir takin' up our hall."

Francis looked up at that. "Forgive me if I'm speaking out of place, but do you think we could get them to help? I mean, I know they've been through a lot, but if some of their people help with the watch and—"

"Ach, you're bloody right," Bette said. "Seher said they wanted ta help, but I said no like the dumb shit that I am. I'll get on that today. Meanwhile, make sure everyone has their eyes open and their weapons close. If young Sharne hadn't been armed to the teeth in her sleep, things might have gone a lot worse."

"Aye," Garrett agreed.

They finished the conversation, and Francis left. Garrett tried to scurry out with him, but Bette hauled him back inside by the collar. "And where do ye think yer goin'?"

"Back to my station!" he protested.

"Ye've been avoidin' me fer days. What's going on? Did ye piss in me boots one night and forget to tell me?"

Garrett refused to meet her eye. "What, ye think I'm hidin' somethin'? Well, I'm not. I'm not hidin' anything. Not a thing."

"Bull. Shit." Bette leaned against the door. "Yer not takin' one step out of this room until ye tell me what's got yer beard in a twist."

Reflexively, Garrett grabbed his beard and stroked it, checking for knots. It was a beard, carefully grown, trimmed, and oiled for years. He was quite proud of it.

He chewed his whiskers. He tapped his foot. Finally, seeing she really did intend to keep him there for as long as it took, he let out a frustrated groan.

"Oh, fer the love of the Queen Bitch, woman! Can't ye let a man come to a thing in his own time?"

"And what kind of a thing would a man be comin' to, eh?" Bette asked, still holding the door closed.

Garrett opened his eyes wide in disbelief. "What kind of bloody thing do ye *think*? I've been mullin' on how to ask ye to be me significant other, ye impossible woman!"

"*Impossible*?" Bette screeched. "Me? *I* wasn't the one runnin' halfway across town just to duck me head and hide from a *lass*!"

"No, yer the one who forced a man into a corner and ruined his plans, is who ye are!" Garrett roared.

"*What* bloody plans?" Bette yelled. "At the rate you 'plan', we'd be old, grey bones by the time ye pulled yer foot out of yer arse and said anything!"

Garrett stepped forwards, his nose inches from hers, hands balled into tight fists. He growled in a low voice, "I have work ta do, so if ye don't mind?"

She stepped forwards and yanked the door open. "Don't let the door hit yer arse on the way out," she snapped.

Garrett stomped out without a backwards glance. He was at the gate when Bette yelled out to him.

"Garrett?" she hollered, fury still simmering in her voice. "Yes!"

"Yes what?" he barked back.

"Yes, I'll be yer girlfriend, ye vertically challenged asshole." She grinned and waved at Tessa, who had stopped in the middle of the street to watch the exchange.

"Thank ye, ye bossy wee control freak!" Garrett hollered back. As he walked down the road, a giant grin spread over his face. "She'll do just fine," he murmured. "Just fine indeed."

CHAPTER SIXTEEN

Julianne stopped pacing to impatiently watch the sun slowly dip towards the distant mountains.

"Jules, you look like you're about to burst," Marcus commented as he saddled his horse.

"Just itching to get this over with," she explained. "I mean, we're not going into battle—at least, I hope we're not—but still, I'll be happier when Adeline is in Tahn, safe and sound with her father."

"I hear you." Marcus finished loading his saddlebags and came to sit by her. "We leave at sundown?"

Julianne nodded, then looked up as Mathias came over.

"I sent Percival out." Hearing his name, the fat pigeon beside him chirped and preened. "No one in sight for miles." Mathias perched on a low tree branch, kicking his legs.

"That makes sense," she said. "Adeline's messages said the town has been closed to visitors since we left."

"You think we can move out early, then?" Marcus asked.

"If there's no one to see us, it seems like a waste of time to hide. Where's Jakob?" Julianne reached out with her mind reflexively. It was the first time she had used her magic that day and it was like a glorious morning stretch. "Ah. Here he comes."

She had brushed Jakob's mind and felt his wet hair and clean beard. He had washed in a nearby stream, then conjured up a magical warmth to dry himself, but was still a little damp.

She had to hold onto her patience as they covered up the campsite and finished readying the horses. By the time they left, the sun was just grazing the horizon.

It was only a short ride from there to Muir, and they arrived at the gates under a brilliant moon.

"Here," Mathias said. "Dismount. The horses will wait for us here." He shook his head as Marcus began to tie his. "They'll stay, and we can leave faster if we don't have to untie them."

Marcus dropped the reins as Mathias cupped his hands around his mouth and a bird-like trill sang out. A few moments later, a fat pigeon flapped down to his shoulder.

"No ties today, Percival. Can you hold it in your mouth?"

The bird cooed and tipped its head to one side. Mathias held out a scrap of paper, and the bird took it, giving it a gentle chew. Mathias grimaced.

"Maybe I *should* have stuck it on your leg. Don't gum it up, pig, and only to the girl, yes?" He let the bird nuzzle his face for a moment before it few off over the wall.

"Right," Julianne said. "Let's do this."

Her eyes turned white as she slipped into the minds of the gate guards.

Both minds were fractured and patched with holes, but functional. They knew they'd been ordered to keep the town closed off, but believed the direction had come from Lord George.

Open the gate. Forget you saw us. Julianne pushed the compulsion into their minds, unworried that it might later be discovered. They would be long gone by then, if it came to that.

The four of them fled through town on light feet, Jakob dulled the noise they made while Julianne cloaked them from sight.

The moon had barely moved when they made it to the manor. "Adeline's rooms are there," Jakob said, craning his neck to point at the fourth floor.

"If anyone would know, it's Jakob," Mathias said with a sly wink.

Surprised, Marcus looked at Jakob. "Really? You and Adeline?"

"What of it?" the big man asked, glowering.

"I think it's sweet," Julianne said. "Like in the old stories. Princess in her tower, wooed by a rough and rugged man with no family to speak of."

"There's more spice than sweet in that relationship," Mathias chuckled, then *whoofed* out a breath as something invisible hit him in the gut. "Do that again, and a whole flock of birds will shit on your head tomorrow," he gasped.

Jakob gave an innocent shrug, but couldn't contain his own laughter. "My lady doesn't like to be kept waiting. What's our plan?"

Four floors up, Adeline eyed the pigeon on her windowsill with terror.

"Yes, of course, father," she said.

"Yes what? I asked *how* you would manage the city while we are away, Adeline. Are you even *listening*?" Using magic to disguise himself as Lord George, Rogan glared at her.

Adeline started. *Dammit, girl, pull yourself together or you'll give yourself away.* "Sorry, father. I was just thinking." She wracked her brain for an excuse. "About... George. I haven't seen George in days. Do you think he's ok?"

Rogan sat back. "I'm sure he's fine. He sent a messenger to say the hunting was extraordinary, and he would keep his men out a little longer. Now, about our journey—"

"Yes, your journey. But, why would you and Rogan wish to travel to Tahn? It's such a small town, and there's nothing there but a few farmers." The pigeon jumped inside, a bit of paper dangling from its mouth.

Oh no. Go, shoo, she thought, knowing it couldn't hear. Still, she wondered if it was being deliberately obnoxious when it began to coo.

Rogan spun. "Get out, you vile—what's this?" He snatched at the bird and missed, but it dropped the note. Rogan ignored the paper, watching Adeline's stricken face as it fluttered to the floor. "Adeline, my love? Perhaps you have something to tell me?"

"What? No, Father. I shall run the city just as you instruct, until you return from your journey." Adeline kept her eyes glued to his face, refusing to look at the stark white scrap on the red carpet.

It was too late. Without taking his eyes off her, Rogan crouched down and picked up the note. Flicking his eyes to it, he read aloud. "Fly, little one. Lover-boy and his rescue party have arrived."

His face darkened. Then, as if her eyes were playing tricks, her father's form wavered and flickered. "Lover?" He took three steps forwards and grabbed her arms roughly. "LOVER?" he screamed, speckles of saliva hitting her face.

The illusion vanished and it was Rogan pinning her down, screaming at her. "You bitch! You evil, lying *bitch*! How *dare* you play with my affection!"

A force shoved at her mind and Adeline struggled to hold it back. Her shielding skills were good, but not as strong as her father or Madam Seher. "You think I could care about a monster?" She spat at Rogan's face, trying to distract his concentration.

The force increased. Adeline's fingers could just brush the small dagger hidden in her belt.

"I *hate* you. Do you know that?" Rogan screamed. "I *hate* you, because you're a *liar*. You've made me angry, Adeline, and that means people will die!"

Got it. Unable to move her arms above the elbow, Adeline could only jerk her hand up to plant the small knife in Rogan's forearm. He let her go and she scrambled back, hitting her head on her desk.

Rogan shrieked. "Guards! Guards, attack!" He held his injured arm close even as he attempted to grab her again with the other. Adeline fell back into the passage behind her desk and kicked the secret door closed. Her shield collapsed.

"Please, be ready," she whispered. She jumped to her feet and ran up the stairs.

Below, Marcus held Julianne's arm as she mumbled urgently. "She got the door open. She's running, upstairs; she can hear someone behind her. There's a tower, she's going—Jakob, catch her! Catch her NOW!"

Marcus jerked his head up in time to see something white and billowing tumble from one of the tower windows. Someone screamed and Marcus realized it was a girl. "Shit!" He yelled and jumped forward, arms out.

The billowing form spun, dress floating in the fingers of wind that caught the fabric. Adeline looked down, seeing the terrified man below. She fell, closing her eyes. Then, she slowed.

It was as though she was weightless, floating down from a height that should have been deadly. Jakob's spell lowered her gently onto the hard, cobbled road, tipping her upright to land steadily on her feet three feet away from Marcus.

"Thanks, but I'm good." She winked at Marcus before throwing herself at Jakob and planting her lips on his.

"Ade!" As he pulled back, Jakob's eyes faded from black to their normal brown. "Thank the Bitch herself."

"*Don't* thank that dumbass bird," she said. "Mathias, I keep telling you, pigeons are morons."

"Sorry, my lady." He grinned in relief.

"Hate to break up the party guys, but we've gotta go." Marcus could hear the rumble of boots on wood floors, building to a crescendo as a nearby door burst open. Soldiers tumbled out, spotting the rescue team almost immediately.

"Go!" he yelled, feet already moving.

Marcus spared a glance back to make sure his companions were following. Jakob pulled Adeline along, Julianne keeping pace. Mathias brought up the rear.

A zing whispered past Marcus's ear. "Bowmen!" he called.

Jakob dropped Adeline's hand and gestured with his fingers. The next volley of arrows froze in midair before clattering to the ground. He reached out again, but groped empty air.

"Already overtaken you, slowpoke," Adeline said.

To his surprise, she was right.

"Stop showing me up," he grunted, then skidded to a stop.

He eyeballed the men hurtling after them, quickly calculating their speed and weight. Then, he raised both hands and made a dipping motion. A wall of flame erupted, barricading the road.

He watched a moment to make sure the spell would hold. The first row of men stumbled, and those behind smashed into them in their haste. The sudden stop sent four rows sprawling on the ground.

"Now, let's spread the love," he whispered. He could hear his companions getting farther away, but didn't move. A twist of his fingers and a click, then the hot, glowing wall flared as fresh flames spread beneath those that had fallen first.

Cotton underclothes and cured leather blossomed into flames. Men screamed and scrambled away, some to avoid the flames and others to try and outrun the ones licking at their clothes.

Jakob grinned, then took off running again. He had almost lost his friends—did, in fact, when they rounded a corner. Taking a breath and crossing his fingers for a good landing, Jakob took a flying leap.

Another hand movement pushed the air behind him, propelling him down the street. He landed, wobbled, then rolled, coming to a stop on his feet. He took a quick moment to balance himself, then dashed down the street his friends had gone down.

"There you are," Adeline scolded.

"I told you he's safe," Julianne said. "Come on. The gate guards are about to be accosted."

They raced for the gates, but got there too late. Almost a dozen men were lined up, crossbows aimed straight at them.

"Duck!" Marcus yelped. No one had needed the warning as the bolts whizzed by without hitting anyone.

By the time the guards had reloaded, each of them had found a doorway or alley to slip into.

The men at the gate didn't approach, but Jakob knew the men he had attacked were only minutes away.

"Jakob, can you get us over?" Adeline said, pointing at the nine-foot wall.

He shook his head. "Sorry. I'm spent."

"We need a distraction, is all," Mathias said.

A loud crack followed by a clatter sounded at the gates. Jakob risked poking his head out. The great oak doors were being pummeled from the other side. Though some of the guards still watched the roads, they looked nervous, and the others now had their weapons pointed the other way.

A bat screeched and dove into the group of men. One man screamed nervously, though the animal hadn't struck anyone.

Then, four bats were flapping at their heads. A minute later the bats swarmed, their high-pitched squeaks drowning out all other noise.

The guards broke formation and ran, some only stumbling a few steps before falling to the ground whimpering and crying.

"Now!" Julianne yelled. Two men, touched by the flapping, scratching mammals, yanked the gate open with a dazed look. "Thanks, boys. Hope you don't catch it in the morning."

They slammed the gates shut once everyone was through. Jakob leaned on the wall to catch his breath.

"No time," Marcus said, pulling him forwards. "Get to the horses."

Jakob nodded at Adeline's worried look. "I'm fine," he said. "But I'll sleep for a week when this is done."

They quickly found their horses and mounted. Jakob pulled Adeline up behind him, and she wrapped her arms around his waist. "Don't let go," he said.

"Why, scared you'll fall off if I do?" she taunted.

"Maybe." He kicked his horse, and they shot through the woods and onto the road.

CHAPTER SEVENTEEN

Bette stood side by side with Garrett, facing down a band of angry soldiers.

"I bloody well told ye, we're not gonna launch a bloody war!" Bette snapped.

"Why not?" Lewis called from the crowd. "You said yourself, they're barely scraping by out there. We only need a few dozen men, and we can take them out forever!"

"Until ye've slit a man's throat while he's got his pants around his ankles, ye've not got the experience to make a decision like this, lad." Garrett spoke calmly, despite his own frustration at the situation.

He knew—they *all* knew—that what remained of George the Third's army was just a short ride away. They had food and tents, but were struggling to survive.

The young nature magician who had scouted for them hadn't kept that as quiet as Garrett would have liked, and now half the town was itching to ride out and give the soldiers a piece of their mind.

Garrett's pride, and the love he had grown to feel for the town, ached to agree. He was a soldier, though. He had been in small scuffles to outright war, and he had seen men die and seen innocents killed.

He knew a massacre was not the same as a fight.

He wouldn't let these people—his people, now—find that out the hard way. They'd already had enough nightmares to last a lifetime. Riding to a one-sided battle wouldn't cure the bad dreams, it would cause more.

"I've said we'll stand down, and I bloody well meant it." Bette ignored the outcry at her words. "No, it doesn't mean they'll get away with it, but the damage at Sharne's was superficial and the man who did it now has a hole in him."

A few cries in support of Sharne went up, until the lady herself waved them down.

"You want to go out there and fight them for me?" she yelled. "They came into my house; they attacked while I slept. That man thought he had an easy target."

The yells rose in volume and urgency.

"You think I'm like him?" She glared at the crowd. "You think I want to lower myself to his standards? If we attack that group, they have no hope of fighting back." She spat on the ground, barely missing one of the loudest men. "You think that's *honorable?*"

The cries for revenge started to fizzle, turning into uncomfortable grumbles as the men stared at the dirt.

"We need revenge," one man was brave enough to yell. Someone next to him elbowed his ribs, and he shut his mouth.

"No," Bette said. "We need to defend our town. When Julianne gets back, then—and *only* then—we can talk about justice."

As a few cheers rang out, she added, "And remember, I said justice—not revenge. Keep that in yer heads while ye stand on watch and sleep in yer beds. We're not a pack of dirty remnant."

"Are ye sure?" Garrett asked her. "I don't think Lewis has showered fer a week, and he bloody smells like one."

Laughter broke up the tension and the crowd dissipated, men moving off to go about their daily business.

When they were alone, Bette jerked her head at Garrett, motioning him around a corner.

"What do ye really think about all this?" she asked when they were alone and hidden from view.

"Well… I'm happier than a pig in shit, but me knees are shakin' like a dog tryin' to shit out a razor blade," he admitted.

She looked at him strangely, then slapped him in the side of the head. "I mean about the army, ye wee horn bag, not yer love life."

"Oh?" he asked, confused for a moment. "Oh! Aye, I knew that. I was jus'… havin' a joke, is all." He coughed to cover his awkwardness. "I'd like ta go out and smack the bastards inta the ground, but yer plan makes sense."

Bette sighed. "If ye feel like that yerself, I suppose we can't blame the men for wantin' ta do the same."

"The men will do as ye say, Bette. They respect ye." He gave her a reassuring grin.

When she kissed him on the cheek, his cheeks flushed bright red. "Aww, yer so sweet when ye blush like a wee teenager," she said, pinching one of them.

His face went even redder. "Stop yer teasing, ye wicked woman. Can't ye see I'm in awe of yer beauty and yer strength?"

She grabbed his face and gave him a real kiss, one long and deep enough to make the tips of his whiskers curl. "Aye," she said when she pulled back. "That's why I love ye." She slapped his ass, then turned around to walk away.

He jumped on her, pulling her back in for a second kiss. This time, it was Bette who pulled back flushed and breathless. "Well, then, I guess we'll call that a tie," she gasped.

"Oh, I'm not so sure. We might need to have a rematch… later, when things aren't so bloody crazy." Garrett grinned, glad to have finally regained an equal footing with her.

"Fair enough," she said. "A rematch, tonight. Make sure ye dress appropriately." Bette turned and walked away, ignoring Garrett's demand to tell him exactly what 'dressed appropriately' even meant.

"Bloody women," he muttered, leaning back against the wall.

"I second that, and raise you 'bloody prostitutes'," Danil piped up as he walked past.

Garrett jumped forwards to join him. "Polly?" he guessed.

"Yup. She's been shadowing me, trying to make herself useful." Danil sighed heavily.

"That… doesn't sound like such a bad thing?" Garrett said, trying to figure out what was really eating Danil.

The blind mystic screwed up his face. "I know! She's being so damn nice, I don't even know what to do about it! Every time I turn around, she's at my heels. I only lost her because I was stupid enough to mention my laundry was piling up, and now she's doing it for me!"

"Don't tell Bette," Garrett warned.

"They're best friends! Polly is going to tell Bette about the washing, and Bette is going to put my head on a pike." Danil's face fell. "How am I gonna get out of this one? I don't even know how I got into it!"

At least Bette doesn't play those silly games, Garrett thought. *Stand in battle by a good woman's side, and she'll respect ye forever.*

Danil stopped in his tracks, reading the rearick's thought.

"No!" Garrett snapped. "Bette said—"

"Bette said we can't wage war on them because it'll be a massacre," Danil said, grinning.

"Aye…" Garrett said warily.

"She never said—"

"Stop!" Garrett yelped, hands up defensively. "Stop, don't say another bloody word, ye bastard. Whatever yer up to, don't tell me."

"Ah," Danil said, smiling. "The old 'plausible deniability' trick? That's fine, but you'll miss the fun."

Garrett shook his head, resolute. "Aye, ye go have yer fun and leave me out of the consequences."

He wondered if he should mention anything to Bette, but Danil was still in his head.

"Come on, Garrett. This is just what I need. Please?" Danil pleaded.

"Ach. Fine. But my name stays out of it, whatever yer plannin'." Garrett cursed his bad luck to get involved with the foolhardy mystic, just when things were going well with Bette, too.

"I won't breathe a word of your involvement," Danil promised.

CHAPTER EIGHTEEN

Adeline rolled over on the thin blanket for about the fortieth time. Sunlight streaming into her face made her mind fight any attempt to sleep. Sticks and small rocks poked through the thin woolen barrier, uncomfortable reminders of all she had left behind.

"You were right to leave," Julianne whispered beside her.

"You don't know that." There was no animosity in Adeline's voice, just sadness. "You don't understand how unstable Rogan has become, how obsessed with me. Now, he's angry, and he'll take it out on everyone around him."

"Will he come for us?" Julianne asked.

Adeline thought for a moment. Rogan could be impetuous and when his fury rose, he would lash out against anyone in arm's—or mind's—reach. Still, when it came to the long game, he was a master of patience and meticulous planning.

"He won't disrupt the plans he has in place," Adeline said with a measure of confidence. "I remember the day Joey, one of Father's clerks, stood up to Rogan. I'm not sure how he got around the mind control, but instead of sending out notices of the new curfew, Joey wrote out notes describing what Rogan was doing, warning people about him."

Julianne waited for her to continue. When the silence continued, Julianne asked Adeline gently if she would drop her shields and show the mystic what happened.

Adeline nodded, a tear leaking down her face. Julianne skimmed her mind for the rest of the sad story.

Joey had distributed thousands of the documents, detailing Rogan's mind control techniques and urging people to resist. He had concluded the note with a line saying his life would now be forfeit.

Behind closed doors, Rogan had flown into a furious rage. He had yelled and screamed, and when that didn't help, he had used mind control to force a guard to smash a huge marble urn with his face.

The guard hadn't survived.

And yet, an hour later, he had taken Joey to the front steps of the lord's manor and thanked him, congratulated him for having the bravery to watch out for his fellow citizens.

Rogan's speech had ever so gently implied that Joey was paranoid, that he been unstable in the days prior. With a gentle smile, Rogan had patted his head and promised that if Joey was so convinced that something was wrong, Rogan himself would submit to any questions he felt the need to ask.

A week later Joey was found hanging from a noose in his room. The townspeople, initially incensed and ready to throw Rogan out on his ass, now doubted Joey's story. They wondered if he had been wrong, or crazy, and if he had killed himself out of guilt or shame.

"What do *you* think happened?" Julianne asked.

"Rogan ordered Joey to do it." Adeline spoke quietly, a tremor in her voice. "I can't prove it—no one can. But you need to know that. You need to know that even though Rogan was angry, *furious*, he still waited. He smiled and sucked up even while he boiled inside, because he knew he had to, to pull it off."

Julianne fell silent, gears turning in her head. "So, he's not likely to come running after us."

Adeline rolled onto her side, watching the young mystic think through the possible ramifications of what they had done.

"Rogan was planning a trip to Tahn. He didn't say when he wanted to leave, but it wasn't immediately. He had a few things to do first," Adeline told her.

"What kind of things?" Julianne asked.

"Well, train me, for one." Adeline waited for that to sink in, then explained. "He was head over heels for me. Maybe because I could block him so well—I don't think he's ever had a girlfriend that wasn't brainwashed into it. I played along so I could get what information I could."

"That was brave." Julianne's heartfelt sentiment cut into Adeline's heart.

Another tear slid down her face, running sideways down to the thin blanket. "I tried, but it wasn't enough."

"Is that how you found out about his fallback plan?" Julianne asked.

"You mean how everyone will die if he does?" Adeline asked.

Julianne nodded. "That one bit of information could save countless lives," Julianne reminded her. "Without it, we would have just lopped off his head, or put an arrow through his chest."

"And now, our hands are tied," Adeline spat. "We're helpless."

Julianne snorted. "He wishes! There's one thing egotistical bastards like Rogan all have in common: they're not nearly as smart as they think they are."

Adeline gave her a disbelieving look. "You don't know Rogan."

"No, but I know people like him." Julianne reached over to squeeze Adeline's hand. "Don't worry, I won't underestimate him... but mental magic is very precise. Words matter, especially for compulsions like that one. If you don't use exactly the right ones, there's usually a way around it."

"So… we might be able to get rid of him without hurting anyone?" Adeline asked.

"I'm sure of it," Julianne asked. "Even if it means locking him in a tower where he can't hurt himself and keeping him there to live out his natural life."

Adeline sighed with relief. "My stomach has been in a giant knot since he told me that. It's nice to feel hope again. Stopping him from hurting anyone will do, even if it means he lives."

"Well, I didn't say that was the most likely outcome," Julianne said. "Because I'll move mountains to make sure that monster gets his just desserts."

"I'll do anything I can to help," Adeline said.

Julianne lay quiet for a moment. "Anything?" she asked.

Adeline nodded. "I'd cut open my soul and make a deal with the devil if it'll help stop him."

"It's your mind I want you to open," Julianne said. "Not your soul. And there's no cutting involved, I promise."

"You're already in my head, aren't you?" Adeline asked.

Julianne hesitated. "This will go deeper. I'll be inside the core of your mind, rummaging around. You won't be able to push me out once I'm there, or shield any part of yourself away from my poking and prodding."

Adeline laughed. "I couldn't shield a fly right now. There's nothing stopping you."

"No," Julianne said dryly. "Nothing except the ethical concerns involved with mind-raping an innocent, unwilling victim." She looked at Adeline expectantly. "This is completely up to you. You can say no."

Adeline stared back. "Mystic, you have my full, unconditional permission to do whatever you want to my mind. If there's information in there that will help you, pull it out. If he slipped any compulsions in there, destroy them. Even if it destroys me."

Julianne turned so she looked up at the sky. Even so, Adeline saw the white film gloss over her eyes as Julianne embraced her magic. With a whispered word, she was in.

Carefully, Julianne combed Adeline's mind for signs of tampering. She followed the pathways of her brain left, right, up, and down. She examined significant memories, and tugged at decision making processes. Finally, satisfied that Rogan hadn't implanted any false memories or orders, Julianne examined everything Adeline knew.

Rogan was everything she had said and more. He was like an overgrown child with a fierce intelligence, but a spoiled nature and no impulse control. Rogan's goal was to rule. Not just Muir, but everything he could touch.

He was impetuous, but also calculating. His downfall was, as in many bad people, greed. His quest for authority over the town consumed him—to the point where it hampered his efforts as they were spread too thin.

Rogan likely could have breached Adeline's shields if he had worked on them long enough, but he was constantly distracted. From conquering Adeline, to amassing an army to go after Julianne, then back to Muir and his desire to squash the local resistance, his goals constantly changed, making it impossible for him to dedicate the focus needed to complete any of them.

Deep within Adeline's mind, Julianne plucked out a memory from the evening before. She didn't hide what she was doing—to Adeline, it was like watching the scene all over again.

Lord George? That must be Rogan in disguise, Julianne thought, the guess confirmed by Adeline's own thoughts. She sank deeper, wrapping herself in the scene.

Rogan, wearing Lord George's face and demeanor, stepped into Adeline's room.

"My dear child, it's so good to see you."

She returned his greeting stiffly. They made small talk, commenting on the weather and the town before Rogan brought up his plans to leave the city.

"I won't be gone for more than a week," he said. "As long as things go well. If my... negotiations are held up, it may be longer."

"Are you going to Wolston?" Adeline asked, knowing he wasn't.

"No, Tahn." Rogan angled a glance at her, watching, but she didn't react. "I wish to recruit more workers there, to help with my plans for the city."

A brief flash, a memory within a memory, showed Rogan talking of building Muir into a utopia, a sprawling city where everyone lived in harmony—under his rule, of course. He already had architects drawing up plans for expansion, but lacked workers to see it to fruition.

"When will you leave?" she asked. "And what of the city while you are gone?"

"It will take another week to prepare my army."

"Army?" she gasped, then quickly composed herself.

"Yes. There have been rumors of bandits. Nothing to worry yourself about, dear." He smiled at her concern. "Now, in my absence, you'll be..."

Adeline's attention shifted to the window. A pigeon sat and cocked its head at her. Anxiety welled as Adeline tried not to pay attention to it.

"Yes, father," she mumbled.

Julianne pulled away. She knew the rest—she had been there for it, leaning gently on Adeline's shield, ready to tumble into her mind to fight Rogan off if it failed.

Relief flooded over Julianne.

"That's good, right?" Adeline asked.

"If you're right—and I think you are—Rogan won't move his plans forwards. It sounds like he's planning a full-scale attack, he'll need the time to get his army ready."

"Oh," Adeline said in a small voice. "So, it's bad."

"It's the best news we could get." At Adeline's dubious look, Julianne explained. "That gives us plenty of time to get back to Tahn and prepare. It's not the defenseless little farming village it was when Rogan first set his eyes on it."

"You really think you can fight off a whole army?"

"No," Julianne replied, unworried. "Just the parts that count."

Satisfied that they had the time they would need, Julianne rolled over and closed her eyes. She sent a tendril of magic towards Adeline, helping the girl to relax her mind and body.

Within minutes, they were both asleep.

CHAPTER NINETEEN

Bastian raised his arm and dropped it. Everyone fell silent. He waited.

Crouched in the woods, black grease smeared on his face and dressed in some of Marcus's spare armor, he wondered how exactly this had happened.

It had been, against all odds, Francis's idea. He had come to Bastian that afternoon, asking for his help to organize a stealth operation against the men who had attacked Sharne.

Bastian, Sharne, Francis, and Mack had snuck out after dark, planning to disrupt the camping army.

"Remember," he whispered. "We're not here to kill anyone. *Anyone!*" he stressed to Sharne, who nodded. "We just want to make them a little unhappy. I'm not half the mystic Julianne is. I can't get us out of trouble if it goes bad."

Their plan was for Bastian to use a sleep spell and control anyone who woke, while Sharne and Mack tipped their water supplies out and stole their food. Francis would light a few smoldering fires before they left. Not enough to burn down the forest, just a few holes in their tents and some ruined supply piles.

Bastian settled back on his heels and let his eyes fade to white.

He brushed against the sleeping men's minds, then moved to the three on watch. He whispered a word, then gently soothed the first man to sleep. When he started work on the second, the target dropped off almost immediately.

He must have been exhausted, Bastian thought. He had never managed a sleep spell with so little effort.

He searched for the third, hoping he wouldn't put up a fight, either. "What the fuck?" Bastian murmured when he couldn't find him.

"What's wrong?" Sharne asked.

"I can't find the other guard." He brushed against the sleepers again. "He's… gone back to sleep?"

Sharne grinned happily, but Bastian shook his head. "Something's not right."

Grass rustled nearby, and they froze. From the corner of his eye, he saw Sharne's spear inch towards the brush. Then, she shoved it forwards.

"Yeowche!" The muffled grunt of pain could only have come from one person.

"Garrett?" Bastian hissed. "What the *fuck* are you doing here?"

"Ye brain-farting douche, why did ye stab me?" Garrett spat back in a loud whisper. "Danil didn't tell me ye were coming, the limp-dicked asshole. I almost stabbed ye in the throat!"

"Danil?" Francis said. "Fuck. Who else have you brought?"

"What? Ye don't know? Hold up." Garrett waddled backwards in the grass, disappearing into the green stalks.

A few moments later, Danil spoke into Bastian's head. *Thought you'd have a little adventure on your own, did you?*

That's not exactly how it went down, Bastian began. Then, he crumbled. *Ok, fine. That's pretty much it.*

What's your plan?

Bastian quickly filled him in. *Did you send the third guard to sleep?*

I did. We tagged one together, too. I noticed you working on him at the same time I was. Danil pulled away for a moment, then returned. *Our plan is a little more... involved. You'll need to cover your faces. When the fire starts to smoke, don't breathe it in.*

What do you want us to do? Bastian asked.

Watch and wait. You can jump in when you get a handle on it. With that cryptic instruction, Danil left Bastian's thoughts.

"Sneaky bastard," Bastian muttered. "I can't believe he slipped past us."

A short distance away, Danil grumbled, "Sneaky bastard. I can't believe he went under my nose!"

"Did ye expect less?" Garrett chuckled.

"He was always the sensible one! Quite proud of him, actually." Danil grinned, then looked over at Tansy and Shell, one of Madam Seher's trainee mental magicians. "We ready, girls?"

They nodded.

"Send in the decoy," Danil instructed.

Behind them, Polly stood. She wore one of Tansy's costumes, a diaphanous gown that, when she stood between Danil and the small, glowing campfire, left absolutely nothing to the imagination.

Polly darted up to the fire, then called out in a soft, melodious voice. "Hello? Hello, is anyone awake?"

A couple of men sat bolt upright, weapons pointed at her before she could blink. One jumped to his feet and grabbed her by the hair.

Others were slower to react. Danil sent gentle waves of emotion out, calming the men to prevent any violent reactions.

Polly pressed a hand to her chest. "I'm so *sorry*. I didn't mean to scare you. I came to ask for your help." Her hips moved ever so slightly, making the dress sway and highlighting her curves.

"Who are you?" barked the man holding her.

"Why, I'm Polly. My carriage was turned back at Tahn, and we didn't have enough time to drive all the way home. I was ready to sleep, but had to step out—*you* know, lady business—when my horse took fright and ran." She giggled. "And me in nothing but my nightdress."

Two more men stood, stepping close. "What'll we do with her, Sarge?"

The sergeant looked suspicious, but one of the men sniffed her hair. "What would you do for us if we helped?" asked the one with the nose.

"Can it, Hoffer," the sergeant snapped.

"You don't own me, Lawson. You lost that power when you ran us into that pisshole, Tahn, and lost us everything." Hoffer aimed his sword at Lawson's gut, but the sergeant didn't flinch. The third man looked on, terrified.

"Stand. Down."

Bastian, sedate the sergeant. Bastian jumped at Danil's unexpected order, then went to work. Sergeant Lawson's eyes began to droop as he swayed on his feet. A yawn cracked his jaw.

Danil sent a sliver of arousal to the two other soldiers. *Go on. Look at her hands. Watch.*

Polly smoothed her dress as she swayed, which really made it look like she was rubbing her hands along her body. Sergeant Lawson didn't object when she pulled away from him, instead clapping one hand to his mouth to stifle another yawn.

She raised her hands to her chest, pushing her breasts up as she fiddled with her necklace.

"I didn't bring any money, but I'm sure I could find something to make you strapping young men feel it was—" she ran a tongue across her top lip "—worth your while."

Danil fed more arousal into the group, then motioned Tansy.

"There's just one more thing," Polly said, tweaking the corner of her mouth into a seductive smile. "My sister is with me." She pressed a finger on the chest of the man who had sniffed her. "Do you think you could help us both… at the *same time?*" She giggled.

A groan escaped his lips as a shudder wracked his body. "I sure could, beautiful," he murmured.

Tansy sashayed up to them, all but unnoticed until she slipped her hands around the second guard's waist from behind. "What about you? Think you can lend a hand to two lost, innocent girls?"

"I... what... uhh, yes, but..." he stammered, red-faced. "Please?" He turned, the motion hiding a quick flick of Tansy's hand towards the fire.

Danil quickly covered his face and motioned for Shell and Garrett to do the same. Both yanked cloths over their heads that were made from dark fabric and painted with ghoulish white faces.

The fire popped and crackled, then roared into the sky. It burned purple, then blue, then purple. White tendrils of smoke reached out, curling in the gentle breeze.

Watching from the sidelines, Bastian held a sock to his face, cursing Danil as he inhaled the odor of damp sweat.

"Will these be enough?" Sharne asked, voice muffled through the cotton scarf over her nose and mouth.

"I hope so," Bastian replied. "If it was anything lethal, Danil would have told us to get out of the way."

Well, he *hoped* he would. The senior mystic was protective, but didn't always think through the potential ramifications of his mad plans.

The men around the campfire were engrossed. They watched the two women, now dancing, in front of them.

Suddenly, Polly spun. When she turned back to them, a mask covered her face. Through the haze of the hallucinogenic smoke, it looked to the men as though she had turned into a rotted corpse.

Your sins have arisen. Your reckoning has come.

The eerie voice whispered through the camp, sending chills through everyone present.

One screamed. Another staggered to his feet, then reeled. A quick boot to the back shoved him into the fire. Polly grabbed the face of the first guard who had leered at her. "Kiss this, sweetheart." She pulled him close to her terrifying mask and he yanked back, screaming.

Weak and unbalanced, he fell back, pulling Polly on top of him. She crawled over him, cackling as she ripped at his pants. "You want me to make it worth your while? I'll cut your dick off and feed it to you, sweetheart."

"Oh, god, get off, please get off," the guard whimpered.

Bow to the might of the Master. Submit while your soul is intact.

The guard, choking on fear, passed out. Polly jumped off as a wet patch spread from his crotch.

"Geez, what a pussy," she said, giving him a hard kick for good measure.

She looked up to see Danil striding through the camp, eyes glowing. A guard stepped up to him, sword raised, then immediately turned and cleaved it through a nearby tent. He stumbled back, dropping his weapon and holding his hands out as if he wanted to throw them away.

Another guard was trying to crawl between piles of food towards the safety of the woods. Polly sprinted, jumped, and landed in front of him, hooded face dangling inches from his. He shrieked and scampered back.

"Light her up, Danil!" Tansy yelled. She whirled two torches in her hands and tossed one into the sky, catching it before it hit the ground. She grabbed Polly. "You ready?"

Polly nodded. She raised her arms and craned her neck back, then let out a howl.

Polly burst into flames. Beside her, Tansy leaped into the air, landing on hands and knees. Lines of fire raced out from beneath her, following the terrified soldiers.

"Run! *RUN!*" Lawson yelled. He grabbed a man dressed in loose cloth and no armor, and hoisted him onto his back. He ran, almost knocking into the burning Polly before reeling back to take another direction.

The limp figure on his back lifted his head. His jaw was slack and eyes dim, but she knew his face.

Polly reached into a boot and took out a small throwing knife. Almost casually, she tossed it after the fleeing guard. It would be some time before Lawson would realize the lord he had carried on his back to safety was already dead, a small, black dagger lodged in his eye.

When the camp emptied, the fire vanished, leaving no damage in its wake. The campsite had been trashed, water barrels spilled and small, real fires smoldering where lanterns had been knocked over.

Tansy sprinkled something over the fire. It steamed, then settled. She pulled off her face and gave an experimental sniff. "All safe," she proclaimed.

"Uhh, how long do the effects last?" Sharne asked worriedly.

"Not long. Once they stop breathing it in, it only takes about fifteen minutes to lose its effect. Unless they figure out what happened, though, they'll be second-guessing everything around them for a while, and the hangover is just nasty." Tansy suddenly narrowed her eyes suspiciously. "Why?"

Sharne motioned her over to behind a shredded tent. Mack lay on the ground, moaning. "Ghosts! Ghosts, and fire that vanished! The spirits exist!"

Tansy let out a peal of laughter. "Oh, no!" She patted Mack on the chest. "He'll be ok, just don't stand in vomiting distance of him in the morning."

Danil came across Francis, glaring at a small fire licking at some food supplies. His lip twitched and one hand clenched.

"Trying to put it out with magic?" Danil asked.

Francis nodded. "Worth a try. It's not working, though."

"Easier way to do it," Danil said. He unlaced the front of his pants and within a few seconds, a hot stream sizzled in the flames as they sputtered out.

Francis chuckled. "Can't say I wouldn't get some satisfaction from it."

"Go on, then." Danil gave him a shove. "There's more to put out and I don't have a bottomless bladder."

"You sure about that?" A voice at his shoulder asked. "Because that's the third pile you've pissed on."

Danil hastily tucked himself in and yanked on the laces. "Polly! I, uhh, didn't see you there."

"That was the point. Tansy's been teaching me to sneak like a cat. Or a cat-woman." She pursed her lips. "Woman-cat?"

"You did well tonight," he said.

She shrugged. "If a girl's got skills, she should use them."

"I didn't know knife-throwing was in your repertoire." They moved away from the soggy food store.

"It comes with the profession. When a guy is trying to dodge his fee while you're flat on your back, a well-placed knife in the door frame may as well slit his pocket on the way past, it spills coin so quickly. Of course, if your accuracy is off, it's more trouble than it's worth."

Danil shook his head.

"You disapprove?" she asked.

"What? No! I just think you've led one hell of a life. You must have a ton of good stories tucked in that head of yours."

"And tucked in there is where they'll stay." She caught his eye. "Won't they?"

"Absolutely." He grinned. "Unless I can pry them out of you some other way. Does the lady have a favorite type of drink?"

Polly put a hand to her chest, feigning outrage. "Why, Danil, did you just ask me on a date?"

He laughed, suddenly tongue-tied. "Well… I guess? That is, if you're not going to stick a knife in my eye for it."

Suddenly, the knife twirled in her fingers. She gave him a sly look, then tucked it away again. "Tomorrow. Right now, I'm dying for bed."

"Sure." Danil shoved his hands in his pockets. Then, he looked up, alarmed. "Wait a minute. Tomorrow I can buy you a drink, or tomorrow you'll stab me in the eye?"

Polly chuckled, a throaty laugh that made his skin shiver. "You'll find out then," she called, picking her way through the campsite to the woods on the other side.

CHAPTER TWENTY

Julianne patted her horse. "Sorry, Cloud. I know you're tired."

The horse let out a disapproving 'harrumph', but let Julianne pull herself up onto the saddle.

"She's fine," Mathias called back. "Just wishes you'd visit her more often when you're not dragging her around the countryside."

Julianne had to admit, she had barely ridden the horse since their arrival at Tahn. In a way, it was lucky—the mare she had taken to Muir on her first visit was still there, probably sold by the innkeeper when he realized she had been left behind.

"When we get back, I'll give you some big, fat carrots," Julianne said. Talking to the horse still made her roll her eyes a little, but the dappled pony had been on her best behavior since she had started doing it.

"Come on, we're nearly home," Marcus said.

They had stopped twice to rest the horses and themselves. Now, night was falling and the chilled air made Julianne wish for a soft bed and warm blankets.

"Marcus, I really think we should make that detour."

He sighed. "I know. I was thinking the same thing."

They were near the spot they had been accosted on the way to rescue Adeline.

"I smell smoke," Jakob said. "But it's not campfire smoke."

Julianne sniffed the air. "You're right." The clean scent of woodsmoke mingled with cooked meat and a sickly sweet burnt smell. "I don't feel anyone nearby."

They turned the horses off the road and headed towards the smoke. It took them a half hour to find it.

"What is that stench?" Julianne asked, holding her sleeve over her nose.

"Smells like stale piss," Marcus commented. He walked over and kicked a stack of soggy ration packs. "Tell you what, I wouldn't be accepting a dinner invitation from these guys."

"Do you think its remnant?" Adeline asked. Despite the filth scattered around, she curiously poked at things. "Wait... this is my brother George's insignia."

Julianne reached out to touch the girl's shoulder. "I don't know what happened here," she said, honestly. "But George... is not in a good way. His mind is broken."

Adeline snorted. "It's not his mind; it's his humanity that's broken. I don't know how Father spawned such a vile little shit, but he did."

"Ah." Julianne wished she could skim Adeline's to see if she was just hiding her grief, but her shields were locked down again. She didn't look worried, though.

"Don't worry, mystic," Jakob said quietly behind her. "Ade hated that little prick. She'll spare no tears over his body when we find it."

"There's no blood here," Marcus pointed out. "Looks like they were scared off, and the campsite trashed after. Unless they did this damage themselves, which makes even less sense."

"Wait..." Julianne's closed her white eyes, holding up a hand for silence. She needed to concentrate. "Someone's out there. Jakob, would you come with me?"

Ignoring Marcus's worried look, Julianne pushed past the brush and into the woods. Jakob followed close behind, hand aloft, holding a warm flame to light the way.

Julianne stopped a little way in, listening. She could hear it now. It sounded like sobbing.

"That's not disturbing *at all*," Jakob snorted.

They soon found the source of the noise. A man, his cotton shirt black with sticky, dried blood, leaned against a tree. "I didn't —" he gasped between sobs. "I didn't mean to let him die. Oh, please, let me die. Let me die," he whimpered.

Julianne shook his shoulder gently. "What happened?" she asked. His mind was too fractured from grief and terror to see what had happened.

The man's eyes opened wide. "Are you one of them?"

"One of who?" she asked.

"The spirits. The ones come to rip my soul open for the sins I've committed." He suddenly jumped up, tearing at his shirt. "Here. Here it is. Go on, do it. Tear me apart; put me out of this misery." When Julianne just stared, he dropped to his knees. "Please!"

She applied pressure to one of his mental pathways. He fell onto the ground and lay still.

Jakob took a step back. "Did you just—with your *mind*?"

"What?" Julianne asked, distracted. "Oh, don't be silly. He's not dead, just asleep."

"Phew," Jakob said as he tipped the unconscious man onto his back.

"No, killing him would drain me far too much." Julianne kneeled down and pressed her hands to his temples, wincing slightly at the smell of old blood and vomit.

She tried to sort through his memories. Snippets floated by, and she touched them, looking for clues.

His lord... ahh, he served Adeline's brother, she thought. *He was in Tahn. Robbing someone. Sharne? Ghosts. He saw ghosts? Wait, that's...*

"Oh, for Bitch's sake!" Julianne snapped. "I'm going to rip him a new asshole when I get home, then break his teeth. He'll be lucky if he doesn't end up a blind-*mute*!"

"What the hell are you talking about?" Jakob asked.

Julianne just shook her head. "Of all the dumb shit things to do, dragging those girls into this was the absolute *worst*!"

"I'm still lost," Jakob complained. He hurried to catch up to Julianne, who was already storming through the trees back to the ruined campsite.

"Mathias, get my horse ready," Julianne called as they approached. "Because if I go near her in this mood, she'll bolt."

"I think *I'm* going to bolt if your ears keep smoking like that," he said, but jumped up to ready the horses.

It didn't take long to circle back to the road, but Julianne had already cooled off by then. Not that she had forgiven Danil's shenanigans—she had just moved from wanting to rip his head off to something a little more considered.

As her fury waned, so did her energy. By the time they reached the gates of Tahn, she was exhausted.

"Oh, who's bloody there now?" Bette yelled down from the small lookout as they approached. When she saw who it was, she hurried down to open the gate. "People think it's a bloody thoroughfare tonight."

"I know," Julianne said in a flat voice.

"Oh. Welcome back, anyway." Bette ushered them through before closing up behind them.

"Jules, why don't you stay in town tonight?" Marcus suggested.

The idea of skipping the long ride out to Annie's was appealing, and would give her an upper hand in the morning, too. "Good idea," she said, just before a yawn cracked her jaw.

"I'll take Cloud for you,' Mathias offered.

Julianne thanked him, then leaned into Marcus for support. "Carry me to bed?" she murmured, face against his chest.

"Really?" he asked, ready to scoop her up.

She shook her head and sighed. "Sadly, no. I need my bitch-boots on for this."

"Your what boots?" he asked, confused.

"For stomping heads and kicking asses." She had already given him a brief rundown of what she assumed had happened back at the camp.

She might not know all the details, but she had figured out that Danil and a couple of the girls from the theatre troupe had snuck in, using mental magic to scare the shit out of the soldiers.

Julianne hadn't told anyone about Lord George's son—that news would have to go to Adeline and her father, first.

She may not have seen the body, but Lawson's memory of plucking out that little knife from his head told her all she needed to know. She recognized the weapon, and, being honest with herself, couldn't blame its owner.

Polly had been George Junior's preferred prostitute. He hadn't been a gentle man, or a kind one. In fact, he was a complete dick-bag. Julianne wondered again how that particular apple had fallen so far from the tree.

Pushing the door to Danil's cottage open with one hand, she made a mental note to herself to get a lock installed. Not because she thought he could be broken into, but because sometimes, small towns fostered a sense of familiarity that could border on distracting.

Danil would need privacy eventually, and if people could just walk on in… Julianne cocked her head at the sound of creaking wood. It wasn't footsteps. Far too rhythmic for that.

When she reached out with her magic, her eyes nearly shot out of her head. *Polly?* She thought, thankful her shields had already been in place. If they hadn't, she would have sent that thought straight to Danil by accident.

Chuckling softly, Julianne pried off her boots and dropped her robe on the table. It was too late to try and find another place to stay, and she sure as hell wasn't walking to Annie's at this hour.

Crawling into a spare bedroom and pulling musty sheets to her chin, she wondered just what she would do with her errant mystic friend.

CHAPTER TWENTY-ONE

Danil yawned and stretched, immediately sending out his magic to see if a pair of eyes was nearby.

When he found not one pair, but two, he almost dove back under the covers.

Don't even bother, I know you're awake, Julianne sent. *Hurry up and get dressed. Polly and I are about to join the theatre crew for breakfast.*

"That's not good," Danil muttered. He reached for his clothes and pulled them over his head. "She sounds way, *way* too calm."

He headed downstairs, almost tripping over his pants in his sleep-soaked daze. Polly immediately averted her eyes.

"Good morning," she said into her mug.

"Um. Hi." He looked at the two women, Polly trying to avoid his gaze, Julianne giving him a blank stare. "Am I... in trouble?" he asked tentatively.

One of Julianne's eyebrows twitched. "Why would you ask that?"

"Because you're looking at me like you want to cut my nuts off and feed them to a dog." He was well and truly in the shit, he

121

could tell. But was it his fling with Polly—unlikely—or his escapade last night?

He embraced his favorite coping mechanism, denial. It *had* to the be Polly thing, not helped by the girl's silence.

Through his magic, he could see the hot steam rising from Polly's cup and occasionally Julianne's furious glare as Polly flicked frequent glances at her. Nothing else. Julianne had him blocked out of her mind tighter than a virgin in a chastity belt.

"Look," he pleaded. "Is this about Polly? Because I swear, I wasn't taking advantage of her. I really *like* her!"

"Danil, apart from your newfound devotion to Polly, is there anything else you feel the need to tell me?"

Oh, shit. She knows. She knows everything. Danil felt a drop of sweat inch down his neck. "What? Oh, that. See, someone snuck into the town and attacked Sharne and her mother. So… we took care of it."

"You… took care of it." Julianne stood, then gave him a bright smile. "Thank you, Danil, for looking after the town so pro-actively. I'm glad you made sure none of the townspeople or our guests were endangered."

He balked at that. *Her smile is too bright. She should be yelling at me for taking the girls. Hell, she should be yelling at me for not keeping an eye on Bastian, too.*

Wondering what kind of torture awaited him, he slowly gathered his things. "So… should we go?"

"I can't wait," Julianne said. Her grin was genuine this time.

Polly stood. "I… just can't," she whimpered, voice choked. She ran out the door, hands over her face.

Alarmed, Danil went to go after her but Julianne pulled him back. "She's fine, I promise. Come on."

"I'll take your word for it," Danil muttered as he walked outside.

The small cottage he had taken over was right by the hall. At this time of morning, the streets were bustling, at least as much as a tiny farming town could bustle. Normally, the people of Tahn would rush about from job to job, used to the mystics that had come to live amongst them.

Today, however, they must have been excited about the return of the mystic master. As Danil navigated the short distance to the hall, he struggled to find a person looking where he needed to go, instead of looking at the two mystics.

Julianne lifted her head high, and the curious watchers suddenly remembered they had somewhere to go.

"Geez, Jules. They really missed you."

"Did they?" Julianne's eyes twinkled as she shouldered her way past a couple of burly performers.

"Good morning, ladies," one said with a bow and a chuckle.

The other one shoved his friend. "Come on. Don't be a tease. Maybe he just likes the breeze."

Danil's brain turned over the exchange as he tried to work out what they had meant. His face turned pink, then purple.

"Julianne?" he said through clenched teeth.

"Yes, Danil?" she answered sweetly.

"Am I wearing a dress?"

"Do you *think* you're wearing a dress?"

He thought back to that morning, his detail-oriented mind going over what he had done.

Woke up. Pulled my clothes on. My clothes? Yes. Went downstairs. Tripped on my... Wait. My pants aren't long enough to trip on. He slapped his face with a palm. "I didn't trip on my pants this morning. I tripped on a Bitch-damned skirt, didn't I?"

Grinning proudly, she nodded.

"Can I at least *see* what I'm wearing?" he begged.

Julianne gave him a skeptical look. "Are you sure you want to know?" she asked.

He nodded, and the patchwork of images he saw through the eyes of others blurred, then refocused. He swallowed.

"I—" voice squeaking, he cleared his throat. "I might just go home and change, then?" He looked at Julianne, beseeching.

She shrugged. "I'm not *controlling* you, Danil. If you want to go—"

He turned and ran, doing his best to cover himself back and front. The soft, see-through cloth of Polly's costume from the night before last slipped beneath his touch, driving home the images he had seen.

Images of himself, walking around in a see-through dress, in broad daylight, in the middle of Tahn.

He tripped on the front and slammed into the door. It swung open and something soft enfolded him.

"Oh, Danil, that was just the funniest thing I've ever seen," Polly breathed into his ear. Giggles overtook her again.

He pulled back, haughtily wrapping the blanket tighter. "You were in on it, weren't you! I thought you were upset this morning. I thought you were *crying*!"

"I was," she choked. "Crying with *laughter!*"

She couldn't take her eyes off him and, through her, Danil could see what he looked like. Furious, proud, and altogether ridiculous.

He tried to maintain his composure, but it was ruined by a loud snort of suppressed giggles. Finally, he let it out.

Throwing off the blanket, he stuck a hip out. He beckoned to Polly seductively, and she screamed with laughter. Tumbling into his arms, she planted a kiss on his lips.

"I'm sorry," she said quietly as she melted into him.

"Don't lie," he said.

"Fine. I'm not sorry in the slightest. Still, I can make it up to you…" She ran a finger down his chest and looped it through one of the ribbons on the dress. "Tonight."

She dropped the ribbon, turned, and walked out the door.

Danil ran to the window. "I'll hold you to that!" he called.

When he finally turned up to breakfast, he was drowned in applause. Rather than shrink away, he played it up, bowing and tipping an imaginary hat.

"Thank you, thank you. Glad to have had the chance to make your stay enjoyable." He winked at Julianne, then went to load up his plate.

"I never knew mystics were so… generously endowed," Tansy said as she loaded his plate.

"Education is our prime objective, so I'm glad you learned an important lesson," he replied.

She gave a pointed stare at his plate, and when he looked down, a fat pork sausage nestled between two tiny potatoes stared back. He nearly dropped it in shock.

"Go on, mystic, sit down," she said, waving a fork at him threateningly.

He slid in next to Julianne. Before she could speak, he waved her down.

"I know what you're going to say. I should have let that army be, and stayed home to focus on our defenses. And I *definitely* shouldn't have taken three women for backup."

"I'd stop now, before you end up naked on a roof somewhere," Julianne said. "Or, I could let you explain to Bette what's so wrong about taking a *woman* for backup?"

Danil groaned and dropped his head in his hands. "I can't get it right, can I?"

"I'd have been satisfied with 'I should have stayed home, Julianne'."

He peeked at her over one hand. "I should have stayed home, Julianne?"

"I'm glad you've learned a lesson. Do I need to have a similar talk with Bastian? I recognized *his* face in one of the memories I saw."

Danil sighed. "No. As much as I'd like to share my pain, he's already terrified enough of what you'll do to him. When he finds out what you did to me, he'll already be praying to the Bitch to spare him."

Julianne speared a sausage and lifted it on her fork. She examined it, then snapped off a chunk with her teeth. "This is tasty," she said.

Pointedly ignoring her, Danil broke open one of his potatoes and layered some butter on it. "So, how'd it go in Muir?"

Julianne's answer was cut off by an eruption of cheers and whistles. She looked up to see Adeline standing at the door of the hall, hand in hand with her father.

Lord George beamed and stood straighter than Julianne had seen him in Tahn. He had left his cane at home and walked steadily, though he leaned on his daughter a little as they navigated the crowd of people that all wanted to speak to them.

Julianne lifted a hand and waved, but Adeline was too busy answering the million questions the troupe threw at her. She was clearly a favorite of all of them, but Julianne could see the lord's daughter was still tired from the long ride.

Come sit with us, we're down the back, she sent, glad to see that Adeline's shields were up, but flexible enough to allow Julianne to mind-speak to her.

Adeline made a beeline for Julianne, tugging her father along behind her. Jakob appeared and whispered in her ear, and she nodded at something, holding up two fingers.

Finally, Adeline slid into a chair beside Julianne. "My goodness, I didn't expect that much of a reception," she gasped.

"Do you want me to get you some food?" Danil asked. "It's the least I can do, now that you're the topic of the day instead of me."

Shooting him a narrow-eyed look, Adeline shook her head. "Jakob is getting Father and me a plate. Why were they talking about you?" she asked innocently.

Danil blushed. "Nothing interesting," he said.

"It was the exact *opposite* of 'nothing interesting', Danil," Polly said. She pulled back a seat next to Danil, then froze when she saw Lord George. "Oh. Um… hello, my lord."

"Polly!" he said with a wide smile. "I did see you were here in Tahn and have been meaning to speak with you. Are you well?"

Uncomfortable with the attention, Polly ducked her head. "Yes, my lord."

"Oh, don't be shy, now. Sit down and eat. No need to worry about me," the old man said.

His congenial tone and relaxed posture put her at ease. She sat, though she poked at her food a bit without eating. "If you don't mind me asking, my lord… how do you know my name?" She had never had him as a client, that was for damn sure.

Brothels weren't illegal in Muir, but they weren't exactly celebrated by Lord George. It was well known his men would come in frequently to nose around the rooms, asking intrusive questions about the girls, the takings, and the customers.

George's face fell. "I know you were… visited by my son, quite frequently. And, I know he wasn't a kind man, wherever he may be now. As much as my men made your lives miserable, their visits were to make sure none of you had bruises or damage from your clients, my son included."

Polly nodded, realizing that fit with the actions of the local guards.

"It's the agreement I have with the madam at Friendship House—I supplied all the medical treatments, no questions asked, but if anyone was rough she was to report it immediately," George explained.

"I had no idea," Polly said, before shoveling a hunk of bread and onions into her mouth.

"I know your profession carries stigma, but I pride myself on taking care of my citizens—all of them," George said softly. "Though, I fear I have failed on a much larger count than I ever expected."

"You haven't failed, Father," Adeline said. She put a hand on his arm. "We'll take back our city. We'll destroy Rogan and make our people safe again."

"I hope so." George gave her a brave smile. "In fact, I don't just hope it will happen. I believe it, too."

CHAPTER TWENTY-TWO

After eating, Julianne left George and Adeline to celebrate the young woman's return with her townspeople.

"Heading off so soon?" Danil asked, following her out.

"We need everyone we can rally to stand with us," Julianne explained. "Or, more to the point, every *mind*."

"Oh. You're going to see Artemis?" Danil scratched his face, wondering if it was too late to disappear.

Julianne nodded, and looped her arm through his. "And no, you can't leave me alone with this. It's too important."

"Come on, Jules. He won't say no to you." Danil didn't resist her pull, but his mind raced for an excuse to leave.

"He's never once said *yes* to me," she reminded him. "Though it would help if Bastian—oh, there he is."

Julianne's eyes shone white and Danil felt the slightest shift in her mind as she reached out to their friend.

"I don't know why he's so reluctant to help," Danil said. "When Little George attacked with his band of armor-clad assholes, he was jumping for joy every time he took one of them out."

Julianne snorted. She hadn't even known the old man was

fighting with them. She knew magic was being used, but had attributed the sudden influx of animal illusions and random fires that did no damage to Danil and Bastian.

Artemis had hidden himself away behind the wall, an old blanket over his head to block out the sun, and thrown illusions and mind control spells into the oncoming army.

He wasn't a particularly strong mental magician, but he *was* smart. His spells had targeted the weakest soldiers, forcing them to flee or to attack their comrades. The whole time, he had been feeding a three-way shield with Danil and Bastian.

"I still can't believe I didn't notice him there," Julianne said. "And I don't know why he won't admit it. Half the damn town saw him there, eyes glowing. Tessa said he would cheer and shout every time he took someone down."

I didn't admit it, because it didn't happen. Artemis sent the shrill mental voice at both of the approaching mystics.

"Artemis, where are you?" Julianne called out in a bored voice. He would have to be in hearing distance—her shield meant he wouldn't have been able to mind-read the conversation.

None of your business.

She turned a slow circle, taking the time to look at the windows of nearby cottages and examine the bushes by the road.

A scrap of fabric floating in the breeze caught her eye. She slowly walked over to the cart. Lying on his back, arms crossed over his chest, lay Artemis. He was cushioned by a pile of loosely stacked grass.

"What are you *doing* in here?" she asked.

"Examining cloud patterns." He pouted at her, then rolled over, gathering an armful of the wilted grass under his head like a pillow.

"Trying to control the weather?" Danil asked with a laugh.

Artemis sat up. "Yes!" He said, eagerly. "You see, the magic users in Holdgate have found a way to change the weather with—"

"I was joking, Artemis!" Danil said.

"Fine. Next time *you* get caught in a storm, don't come running to me." Artemis turned to glare at Danil.

When have I ever gone running to him because of a bit of rain? Danil thought. He was, for a change, wise enough to keep it to himself.

"Artemis, may we speak?" Julianne asked gently.

"No." He burrowed further into his grassy bed.

"Julianne!" Bastian called. "I wondered where you'd got to. What are you—Is that Artemis?" he asked as he came close enough to see into the wagon.

"Go away." The old mystic sat up, shook the grass off, and spat some green strands out of his mouth. "Better yet, stay. I'll go, before you can try and talk me into some ridiculous scheme that might just get me killed."

"But Artemis," Bastian quickly said, before the others had a chance to speak. "You're the town hero! If you're not there, who will the villagers look up to? How will they know they're safe?"

To Julianne's absolute shock and amazement, Artemis paused. He looked back at Bastian suspiciously. "They can fight," he said uncertainly. "And they have *you* lot to do the mind magicking stuff." He flapped his hands around his head for emphasis.

"Artemis, they don't trust us like they do you," Bastian pleaded. "They know you're smarter than all of us put together."

Artemis preened a little at that. "Well, I *am* quite intelligent. This many years of study can't be done in a day, you know."

"Just *think* how much you'll be celebrated for saving the whole town not once, but twice," Bastian pressed. "You'll have so many pies they'll start leaking out of your ears!"

At the mention of pies, Artemis grinned. "They *have* been giving me a lot," he said. "I suppose… If I were to help out, just a little, and from a very safe distance away… how many more do you think I'll get?"

"More than you can eat," Danil promised. "And of course,

when Lord George awards medals for the bravest and most honored fighters, you'll be there to receive one, won't you?"

Danil? Did you just promise something on Lord George's behalf that he knows nothing about? Julianne sent the thought directly to Danil's mind, shutting Artemis out of the conversation.

He'll be fine with it, Danil sent back. *Especially if he thinks it was your idea.*

Julianne rolled her eyes. *Fine. But* you're *the one who'll have to explain it to him.*

Danil grinned suddenly. *We could make it a real event!*

"So, can we count on you, Artemis?" Julianne asked, cutting off Danil's train of thought. "Rogan will be here within the week, and we need to know you'll have our backs."

Artemis hesitated, so Bastian spoke up. "Of course, he will. He wouldn't want the people of Tahn to think he was scared. They might stop plying him with food!"

That made the old man's mind up at last. "Fine. I'll help with your horrible plan. Don't blame me when you all get yourselves killed, though. And don't expect me to share any pie!"

Making a show of turning his back on them, Artemis stomped off. He didn't get far, confronted by a fine spiderweb, glistening with tiny dew drops. Something about it caught his attention and he dropped to the ground, legs crossed, staring at the web as his fingers twitched, and he began to mutter long winded theories about the nature of water, evaporation, and rain.

"Aaannnd we've lost him," Danil said.

He spoke loud enough that Artemis should have been able to hear, but the old mystic didn't react.

"At least he's agreed to help us," Julianne said.

"You really think he'll come through?" Danil asked.

Bastian laughed. "You underestimate the power of pie. He'd fight the whole battle alone and agree to host a month's worth of dinner parties if you offered him enough of it."

"Fair enough," Danil said with a sigh. "Speaking of battles, I've been hearing some really strange rumors about Bette and Garrett."

"You mean the one where they were screaming at each other in the streets and somehow ended up dating by the end?" Bastian laughed. "Yeah, I heard. It's just crazy, small-town gossip, though. Right?"

"No, it's not," Julianne said. When the two men looked at her in shock, she just shrugged. "Bette told me. She was mad it took him so long, and he was terrified to ask her. You know what Garrett's like when he's scared of something, all blustery and arrogant."

"No, I *wouldn't* know what Garrett's like when he's scared," Danil pointed out. "Because I still haven't found anything that scares him."

"Except women," Bastian said with a laugh.

Danil snorted. "Point taken."

He pulled out a waterskin and took a mouthful. Bastian's eyes flashed white for a moment, then Danil passed the water to him.

"Danil, seeing as you're so eager to talk about relationships..." Julianne began, cutting him a look.

"Ok! Fine, I'll stop." Danil held his hands up, a look of terror etched on his face. "Not another word, I swear."

"Oh, lighten up." She swatted him in the chest. "I was just going to say that I think you and Polly are *adorable* together."

Water sprayed the ground as Bastian choked. "What? Polly?"

At Julianne's warning look, he bit his lip and tried to stifle the chuckles.

Oh, stop! Julianne sent urgently. *He's incredibly sensitive about it.*

Oh, I bet she knows all *his most sensitive spots,* Bastian sent back, then started laughing again at his own joke.

It was Julianne's turn to try and hide a smile.

"What?" Danil demanded. "I *know* you're talking about me."

"Never said a word," Juliane said. She rubbed her nose and coughed, trying to hide her laughter.

Danil threw his hands up. "Do you hate me today?" he demanded. "First you put me in a dress, now this?"

"Wait. *Dress?* Oh, come *on!*" Bastian cried out. "The *one* time I miss breakfast!"

"You… you…" Lost for words, Danil threw his hands up in the air and walked off.

"The dress story will have to wait," Julianne said. "Mathias needs to see me. No poking fun at Danil!" she warned as they headed in separate directions.

"Julianne!" Mathias called out, raising an arm to catch her attention.

"Mathias, what's wrong?" she asked.

"A bird came in," he said. "From one of our contacts."

Madam Seher had left a few people back in Muir, supporters that were sending regular updates to Tahn through Mathias's birds.

Julianne's muscles tightened in anticipation. She couldn't read the information from the druid's mind, but the crease between his brows and the stern set of his mouth made it clear the news wasn't good.

"Here. Quicker if you read it." He thrust the scrap of paper at her.

Lord George told all of Muir that Adeline was captured by Tahn rebels. Seher made to look like instigator. Calling for volunteers to lead fight.

"That cunning bastard," Julianne said. Rogan might be an evil prick, but he was clever.

"Right. Using the innocents for cannon fodder? He knows George and Ade wouldn't ever hurt their own people." Mathias tucked the note back in his pocket. "At the same time, what's to stop us putting Adeline up on the wall? If they see her, they'll know he's lying."

"Illusions," Julianne said, thinking it over. "He'll cast illusions to disguise her, or hide her somehow. Or, if he's as devious as I think, he'll wait until she's up there, and create an illusion that makes it look like she's screaming for help, or show us killing her in front of them."

"If the people of Muir thought they saw us do that, they'd burn Tahn to the ground," Mathias said. "Damn. What do we do?"

"Beat him at his own game," Julianne said with a grin. "He's not the only illusionist this side of the Madlands, you know."

"I'm glad you're confident," Mathias said with a relieved smile.

"I am," Julianne said. "Not just that he won't win… we're going to grind Rogan into dust and feed it to the pigs for breakfast," she said.

Mathias raised his eyebrows. "Remind me never to get on your bad side, ok?"

"...and when they drag beloved Lady Adeline out in front of all those people, all those insipid, wailing city-dwellers, we'll cast a little illusion ourselves," Rogan spat, pacing up and down in front of his throne.

"You'll hide her?" Donna asked, voice laced with skepticism. "Make her look like a donkey, perhaps?"

"We'll make a knife appear, and blood will gush from her throat. She will collapse. In the frenzy, not one of them will notice if she spits in their face, alive and well." Rogan turned cruel eyes on the guard that watched them.

The guard was already pale, listening to Rogan's plans for Tahn. When he saw the new master of the city was looking his way, he almost shat himself.

"Find this talk fascinating?" Rogan asked.

"N-no, my lord," the guard stammered.

"Cut out your tongue," Rogan said in a cold voice. "Wouldn't want any chance of our plans to get out."

The guard sucked in a quick breath. He reached for his knife.

"Rogan, do you really think that's warranted?" Donna asked.

She didn't particularly care what Rogan did to his victims, but she would rather it not be done in front of her. "The mess will be horrendous and the stink of rotting blood will hang around for days."

Rogan sighed. "Fine, stop."

The guard froze, his tongue pinched between two fingers, the knife already ripping with a thin stream of blood. To his credit, he hadn't screamed yet.

"If you ever open your mouth to speak of what I have planned, *then* you will cut your tongue out."

"Yeth, Mathter" the guard lisped. His lips were stained red and a small, crimson dribble escaped his mouth as he spoke.

"For fuck's sake, go clean yourself up." Rogan waved his hand, dismissing the guard, who fled the room as fast as he could. "Idiot."

"Why do you insist on chasing this particular rabbit?" Donna asked.

Her words were calm, controlled. Inside, she seethed, boiling with angry contradictions.

Why should he care about those bitches? she wondered. *Why should he chase them down when he has me? Because they need to die, that's why. But... He's weak, he won't kill Adeline. He loves her. I don't care. I don't care who he loves.*

She twitched, the internal monologue twisting her brain until it hurt.

Yes, you do. The sudden thought made her jump. She couldn't tell if it was her own or if Rogan had slipped it in there without her realizing.

Aloud, she asked what his plan was if Julianne somehow succeeded in convincing their people that Adeline lived.

"Kill them," he said, as if she had asked what to do with spilled tea. "My loyal guards are well and truly bound, now. The rest are paid well enough not to question my orders."

"And then?" Donna asked. "What will you do once you've wiped Tahn from existence and killed the women who defied you?"

She bit her cheek, admonishing herself for even asking. *He's not going to tell you his happy ending involves you,* she thought viciously.

"Kill them? Oh, no. Adeline will not be killed. Her people need her! They need a figure to look up to, someone to tell them everything will be alright. I'm afraid I'll have to break her mind, but I won't kill her." Rogan stopped pacing and flopped into his chair.

A shard of ice slithered through Donna's gut. "You'll keep her as a pet?" she asked coldly.

"As my wife." Rogan darted a glance her way. "You didn't think *you* had a chance of that, did you?"

"I simply live to serve. I have no greater goal than that," Donna said in a flat, emotionless voice.

"Wonderful. Now, about our army. You got the information I asked for?"

She had. Donna rattled off a long list of numbers: the soldiers they had, those they had lost when George's son disappeared, the number of days they could feed them, how many carts would be needed to transport the food, how many more they could get within three days.

Rogan listened intently, mind running over his plans. They would march on Tahn in four days, an army amassed through his lies and his magic mind tricks. They would send the citizens of Muir against the gates first.

When the fool mystic girl brought out Adeline to parade her before them—and he knew she would—they would hammer the last nail in their coffin themselves. With Adeline supposedly dead, slaughtered before the very eyes of her avengers, he would call to attack.

The mystic bitch would come for him, if she wasn't trampled by the very people she was trying to protect. Rogan closed his eyes, losing himself in a memory. It was the only time he had truly seen her, standing proud and strong against his magic.

She hadn't shown fear or groveled at his feet like so many weaker men and women. Julianne, just like Adeline, had faced him proudly. Then, she had tricked him. Her illusions were perfectly crafted, showing a strength of power and quickness of mind he envied.

I will own you, he thought, imagining he could send the words straight to the girl's mind. *I will own you and make you dance for me. Perhaps, in front of your soldier friend? We can watch him squirm together.*

Donna's whining voice brought his attention back to her. "Yes, yes." He waved his hand, dismissing her. "We leave in four days, no matter how many men, or horses, or useless fucking carts we have. If there's not enough food, we'll make them forget they're hungry."

"Even if they don't feel it, they'll still fall over dead if you starve them," Donna pointed out.

Rogan could swear there was a thread of haughty condescension to her, something that hadn't been there since he had broken her. "You presume I care. We'll ride them hard, fight them until they're dead. If they're not strong enough to make it back, I don't want them."

Donna glared at him.

"Go. Your face irritates me," Rogan snapped, unsettled at her sudden change in demeanor. He checked the spell latched onto her mind and breathed a sigh of relief to find that it was still intact.

Donna swept out, leaving Rogan alone.

All too often, he was alone. "What would you do if you were here, little Julianne?" he asked the empty room.

"I'd kill you, Rogan," he replied to himself in a high, squeaky voice. "I'd use my pretty face to distract you and cast my magic."

"And when I beat you?" he asked, voice deep again.

"I'll fall at your feet and worship you, Master."

Rogan smiled down at his imaginary foe. "That you will, girl. That you will."

CHAPTER TWENTY-FOUR

Arnold slowly approached the tall, white wall. He held a flimsy stick aloft, twitching it to fan out the scrap of shirt that hung from it. The fabric was torn and muddied, but still, he hoped, recognizable as white.

"Who's that?" someone yelled, voice muffled by the barrier between them.

"My name is Arnold!" he yelled back. "I've come to negotiate the surrender of my men."

He supposed they were his men, now. Lawson was gone, their lord dead. Arnold was the highest-ranking officer left and, though his honor was likely in tatters from this cowardly move, his sense of right allowed him no other choice.

The soldiers he now led were dying. They were starving, their food supplies lost to whatever the hell had attacked their camp and fouled the supplies. Diarrhea was rife and three of his charges—of the seven that were left—and were now too weak to stand.

He might be a coward, but at least his men would live.

A gate screeched open. "Well? What are ye waitin' for?"

Arnold squinted, wondering why the stocky man who spoke

to him had the voice of a woman. When he got close enough to see the musclebound girl, he swallowed. Perhaps, then, that rumor was true.

His men had sworn they had faced down women on the battlefield. Not just one, and those they had seen fought like demons.

It was no secret his lord's sister, Adeline, had convinced their father to overturn the law that prevented women from joining the army and guards, but George the Third had never had an applicant that met his standards.

Women, he had said, were just not built for fighting.

"Keep yer eyes up here, soldier," the woman snapped as he reached the door.

Arnold blushed, realizing he had been staring at her chest. Not lustfully, but wondering how a tiny farming town had sourced such high quality armor.

He dropped a glance to her sword. No, he realized. That wasn't made here. She must be a foreigner.

It would explain her odd manner of speaking, at least.

Rough hands grabbed Arnold and held him still while a tall, blonde man patted him down. His movements were trained, precise, fingers darting into boots and gripping his sleeves firmly enough to discover any weapons.

He carried none, but the process was a clear sign that he was not dealing with amateurs. He hoped the man wouldn't notice his trembling knees.

"Enough, Marcus. His intentions are honest."

Arnold twitched his head to see a woman robed in white watching them.

She stepped forward and bowed her head to him slightly. "My name is Julianne. I'd offer you my hand, but I understand there's been illness at your camp?"

"Yes, there—how did you know?" Arnold asked, suddenly afraid.

"I'm sorry. I'm a mystic—I read your mind while you waited outside.

He had heard of such things. The theatre performers were rumored to use mind-magic in their performances, and every now and then, a rumor about Lord George's advisor would cross his path. Those stories were enough to make his toes curl.

Julianne waited for him to process the information. "So… you know why I'm here?"

"Yes," Julianne said. "And we accept your terms."

"We do?" the tall soldier asked.

"Yes, Marcus. Arnold here would like to submit his men to our mercy. He asks only that we treat them fairly and, if we put them to death, we do so quickly and cleanly."

"Wow." Marcus looked at Arnold with new respect. "Must be really bad out there."

Arnold shrugged. "We'll all be dead in three weeks, I imagine. I'd rather a knife at my throat than to shit myself to death, spending three days on my back waiting for it to happen."

Marcus took a step back. "Ah. *That* illness." He wiped his hands on his pants, face screwed up in distaste.

Arnold nodded. "It started with hallucinations. All of us, delirious. Then came the vomiting, and just when we began to recover, the shitting started to take us, one by one."

Several people cleared their throats and looked away, but Arnold ignored them.

"If you surrender, wholly and completely—and we will know if any of you are lying—you may join us," Julianne told Arnold. "We'll offer medical care, food, and clothing. You will not take anything not given to you, and once you are well, you will fight for us if we ask it."

"Fight against my city?" Arnold asked.

"Fight *for* it," Marcus said. "We're not out to take your city, you idiot. Our target is Rogan, and he's done more to hurt Muir —and Tahn—than anyone else."

Arnold gave a curt nod, shoulders slumped in defeat. "Fine. But please, one of my men is on his deathbed. If you plan to let us live, I beg you let me go for them now."

"We'll bring horses," Marcus said. "Mathias?"

A thin man stepped out from the watching crowd. "I'll get them. How many men?"

"Seven," he said.

Julianne's face fell. "I'm sorry for your losses," she said, genuine feeling in her voice.

Arnold shrugged. "It's the price of war. Nothing less."

Mathias soon returned with a half-dozen horses. "This is all I could find," he said. "The sick men can ride back. We'll travel on foot."

"Take Bastian," Julianne said. "He could do with a walk."

They set off, coming to the pitiful group just beyond the tree line.

"Ack, it smells like a shithole," Marcus said, gagging. "Only with more shit, less hole."

"I told you," Arnold said. "They're not well."

That much was obvious. The men were lethargic, their skin varying shades of a sickly blue-grey and more than one pile of vomit on the ground.

Bastian stood back, his shirt pulled up over his nose to mask the odor.

"Foraging in the woods, were you?" Mathias asked them with a grin.

"Nothing unusual," one of Arnold's men said. "Just some fruits and a couple of rabbits we caught."

"And who brought back the Bear's Grapes?" Mathias squatted down, poking a finger at the small pile of nuts and berries left on a tree stump.

"The red things?" another man asked. "Gant. He said they were safe!"

"And where's Gant now?" Mathias asked.

Mumbling from the men revealed Gant was the first to shit and vomit himself to death.

"Never trust a dead man when it comes to wild berries, folks." Mathias ran his eye over the miserable group, then picked out one man who lay on his side, watching but not responding.

The soldier's eyes followed Mathias, but he didn't react when the druid leaned down to press his fingers to the sick man's face. Mathias breathed in and his eyes turned green.

When he pulled back, the sickly tinge had faded and his patient sat up, looking brighter, if not entirely better. "What did you do?" he asked in awe. "It doesn't hurt anymore."

Mathias shook his head. "Bunch of idiots," he muttered under his breath. He gave a second man a partial healing, then deemed the rest fit to ride.

"I'll dole out healing as it's needed, but I'd rather not do it standing in a puddle of puke," he said.

"Come on, you heard him," Arnold said.

He and Marcus helped get the sick men onto horses while Bastian slowly walked through the group, his eyes white. Each time he passed one of the men, he would pause, concentrating. Then, he would nod and walk on.

Once he had examined all of them, he stood off to the side and gestured for Marcus to join him.

"They're all good to take back?" Marcus asked him quietly.

"They'd all sell their souls for a warm bed, and a clean bathroom. If we treat them well—or, honestly, as long as we don't threaten them outright—I think they'll do as we ask, and respect the treaty."

Bastian watched as Arnold herded his men into a tight group, then looked to Marcus for permission to set off. Marcus gave him a wave, and the horses slowly plodded off, Arnold leading them on foot.

"What do they think of their new leader?" Marcus asked.

"They respect him. More than his commander, in fact."

Bastian frowned. "Look, these guys aren't particularly smart or especially brave. But, given a *good* leader—not the shitheads they've had so far—they could do good things."

Marcus chewed on that for a bit, then went to speak with Arnold himself.

"Are you well enough to walk?" he asked, noticing Arnold's pale face, damp with sweat.

He nodded. "Well enough. I haven't had the shits, not yet, anyway."

"Why did you wait so long to come for help?" Marcus said. "And why aren't you sick?"

Arnold dropped his head. "George… he made us think you were all traitors. He said your leader, Julianne, was out to take Muir and would kill any of us that tried to defect. Not that we would have."

"Sounds like a douche," Marcus said, matter-of-factly.

"He was an a-grade asshole. But we're soldiers. We fight for our lord, no matter what." Arnold squinted into the late afternoon sun, then turned back towards Muir. "We thought we were honorable."

"Honor can be a complicated thing," Marcus agreed. Then, he said, "Or, it can be dead simple. Do right by people. You do right by people, all the time, and your honor will stay intact."

"Did I do right by surrendering?" Arnold asked. "I pledged to give up my men to the enemy."

"Would you have led us to them if you thought we would string them up and torture them?" Marcus asked.

Arnold shook his head violently.

"So, you faced professional embarrassment and loss of your ranks if you ever return to Muir. You risked what little you had left to save the lives of your men." Marcus grinned. "Seems pretty honorable to me."

Arnold sighed in relief. "Thank you. As for your other question… well, I was faced with watching my men starve. I rationed out the food, but didn't take any for myself." He grimaced. "I thought I was doing them a favor."

"Rather have a stomach not fed than one forcefully evacuated?" Marcus laughed. "You did a good thing, and it worked out for you. Don't feel bad about it."

"If you say so." Arnold didn't seem convinced, but he let the matter lie.

They travelled back to Tahn slowly, stopping every now and then so that Mathias could check on the men. He administered healings when needed, but spared himself as much as he could.

"How are you feeling, Mathias?" Marcus called after their third stop.

"Nothing a mug of that nice Tahnish mead won't fix," the druid called back.

"No more rest stops until you get that, hey? I'd like to make it past the gates by dusk." Marcus didn't say it out loud, but the druid looked tired and Marcus didn't want to wear him out in case he was needed elsewhere.

"Don't worry about him too much," Bastian said. "Druids don't tire as easily as mental magicians. They have ways of replenishing their energy."

Marcus just shook his head. "I don't even know what that means. If you say he's ok, I believe you."

Bastian laughed. "This, from a man I would bet my balls has a talent for mental magic."

"Me?" Marcus snorted. "That's the most ridiculous thing I've heard since we started this journey. And we've seen some weird shit!"

It was Bastian's turn to shake his head. "You have a natural, untrained shield. There *has* to be some magic in you, you're just too set in your ways to access it."

"Damn straight I am," Marcus insisted. "I don't want it. I don't even want to know about it! As much as I appreciate having the ability to keep my girlfriend from reading my thoughts, I—" he cut off abruptly, realizing what he had just said.

"Does Julianne know she's your *girlfriend*?" Bastian teased.

"It was a figure of speech!" Marcus protested.

"Not a word from me," Bastian said. Just as Marcus was about to thank him, he added, "But thoughts? Now, that's a whole other story."

Marcus let Bastian walk on a little ahead. Then, he reached into the saddlebag of a nearby horse. The mare didn't flinch, nor did her rider as he pulled out a pair of wadded up socks.

Marcus gave them a quick sniff. *Yep, they stink,* he assured himself. Then, he lobbed them at Bastian's head, the damp, smelly ball thumping him on the back of the head.

"Hey!" Bastian yelped and turned around, hand clutching his head. "What the hell was that?"

"Just enjoying my magical ability to block out mind reading smartasses," Marcus taunted.

"Oh, that's it." Bastian screwed up his face, eyes white. He whispered a word and something slammed into Marcus's shield.

Accustomed to brute force attacks after training so often with Julianne, Marcus resisted. He breathed slowly, focusing his mind on repelling the attack.

The horse beside his walked, its steady, clopping hoofbeats striking a rhythm with Marcus's heart. As the pressure on his mind increased, so did his resistance.

The world shrank to his own boots, one foot hitting the hard ground as another lifted up to take the next step.

The sun on his neck. The shuffling people. All of it narrowed in his mind to bolster his shield.

When an icy cold stream of water poured down his back, Marcus squealed. "What the utter *fuck*?" he shrieked.

Behind him, Bastian burst out laughing. "Yeah, soldier. You try blocking *that* shit out of your mind." He slipped his waterskin back into his belt as he tried to catch his breath.

"Why did you do that, you fucking sadist? I'm drenched!" Marcus could feel the water dripping down his ass crack and leaking down the leg of his pants. He was soaked, from the back of his neck down the the trickle of water pooling in his boots.

"Lesson one: never assume a mental magician will only use mental magic against you." Bastian lifted one finger up, then added another. "Lesson two: as a mental magician, always make sure you have moves to rely on that don't use magic."

"Let me guess, your esteemed Master Mystic taught you that?" Marcus asked through clenched teeth. He shivered as a cool breeze touched his wet skin.

"Of course!" Bastian said, cheerfully. "She *is* the best, you know."

"Admit it, lad," Mathias said with a chuckle. "He won that round."

"This round, maybe. Next time?" Marcus shook the water off and started walking again. "Better watch your back, Mystic!"

By the time they returned to Tahn, Julianne had mobilized the townspeople. Men and women bustled back and forth, clearing out one of the barns near the center of town. Sharne greeted them at the gate and led them to it.

"The weather is mild enough that it shouldn't be uncomfortable, and we found enough beds for all of you," she said flatly.

They reached the barn and dismounted. Mathias led the horses away as Sharne pushed open the barn doors. It was only when he saw the flood of light inside the old building that Marcus realized the sky had turned purple and the air chilled.

Duty done, Sharne let the door swing shut behind Arnold, the last to enter.

"You ok with this?" Marcus asked.

"I don't have a choice, do I?" she asked.

He could see the angry set of her shoulders, but she didn't let it show on her face. Still, if Marcus had been made to provide refuge to someone who had attacked him in his sleep, he didn't think he would be too happy about it.

"Bastian said they're not bad men," he reassured her. "They were just under some shitty leaders. Those are now dead, and these guys are itching for a second chance."

"Dead?" Sharne asked.

Marcus nodded. "If the man who attacked you was among them, Bastian would have noticed, and said something."

Sharne thought about that, then nodded. "If I *do* see the guy who broke into my house, I can't promise he won't end up with a spear through his other leg," she warned.

"Fair enough." Marcus put an arm around her shoulders. "In fact, if I see the guy, I'll hold him down while you do it."

"What makes you think I'd need you to?" she quipped.

CHAPTER TWENTY-FIVE

Francis glared at the yellow rag, tied to a stick poking out of the duck pond. He looked around again, making sure none of the feathered residents were nearby.

"Focus," Trini said beside him.

Trini was a fire user, and one of Madam Seher's performers. Why she had agreed to take time out to teach Francis, he didn't know. He wasn't about to look a gift horse in the mouth, though.

He pushed out a fast, hard breath, eyes on the fluttering cloth.

"Now," Trini said. "Reach deep inside. Tug on that anger, or whatever juices your lemon. Gently, mind—you don't want to blow it up, just start it smoldering."

Francis gently pulled up a memory of the army that had attacked Tahn. The fear of seeing the army and the exhilaration of the fight fanned his emotions and made his heart pick up speed.

He let it fuel him while his eyes strained to bore a hole through the end of the stick. He stared so hard his eyes blurred, and the stand of trees in the distance became hazy.

"Look!" Trini clapped her hands excitedly. "You did it! *We* did it! I've never taught anyone before. I didn't think I could!"

"You… didn't?" Francis squinted and realized his eyes weren't blurred. A tendril of smoke rose from the cotton rag and a dark edge lined a jagged hole in it. He watched it cool and dissipate.

"How do you feel?" Trini asked. "You're not tired, are you? Did you overdo it? Shit, Julianne will have my ass if I push you too hard."

"I'm fine," he reassured her, though he couldn't quite tell if his legs were shaking from the exertion, or excitement. "Can I try again?"

She leaned in close, checking his eyes and holding the back of her hand to his forehead.

"I guess. It's not your first time, right? Bastian said you've set some pretty big fires." Trini stepped back to give him some space.

"Uhh, yeah." Francis blushed, hoping Bastian hadn't told her he had almost burned a barn down by accident. "I just couldn't control it properly."

"Control is *everything*," Trini explained. She folded her legs up and sat on the ground to watch. "If you don't learn to pull back, you can burn yourself out. Well, not *literally* burn. I haven't seen that happen, though I *suppose* it could, in theory… but you can end up an empty husk if you're not careful."

"I'll keep that in mind," Francis said.

He tried to copy what he did before and this time, he noticed the smoldering cloth before Trini did. The edges of the burning end glowed and he clenched his hands, breathing fast.

Acting on instinct, he splayed out his fingers in a burst and a flame sprang up, shooting to the top of the fabric, then dying as it ran out of fuel. A scrap detached and floated down, sizzling and smoking as it hit the water.

"Woah!" Trini scrambled to her feet. "It took me weeks to be able to do that! I mean, I was only seven at the time, but still!"

"You were *seven*?" Any pride Francis had at his sudden leap in learning dissipated.

Trini laughed. "Yeah. Special case. My aunt knew Seher from

way back, so when I started playing with fireballs as a kid, they shipped me off to her straight away."

"They sent you away because you were blessed?" Francis asked, disbelieving.

"Well… it was more because I kept burning holes in my bedsheets," she laughed, unworried about her parents' choice. "It meant I grew up with magic, and I spent all day, every day practicing. I think Seher was afraid I'd burn her tent down if I didn't get a handle on it fast."

"I guess. You don't miss your parents?" Francis asked.

Trini shrugged. "I visit twice a year. It's fun, and I'm always glad to be back for the first few days. But Francis, have you *seen* what we do? Travelling all over, performing for people? It's like, every kid's dream, and we do it *every day!*"

Francis shook his head. "I've seen some of the tricks you all do for the children, but we don't really get many theatre-people around these parts."

Trini's eyes nearly fell out of her head. "You've never seen a performance?"

Francis frowned. "Well, there was that group that had puppets, but that was more for children. And the Queen's Theatre. They mostly just lectured us about our sins and how Queen Bethany Anne was going to come and send us all to hell."

"Oh, you poor, deprived, art-starved man." Trini leaped to her feet. "This is serious! I need to fix this."

She took off running, then stopped and turned back. "Keep practicing!" she yelled, before taking off again in the direction of town.

Francis just shook his head, bewildered at her sudden disappearance. He turned back to the stick and realized there was nothing but a scrap of black thread left.

"I suppose I had better do what she says," he muttered.

He tore a strip off his shirt. It was an old one and destined for the scrap pile anyway. He slipped off his boots and gingerly stepped into the cold water. As he waded out to tie the fresh cloth onto the stick, he let himself imagine where this could lead.

When he had wet his feet tying Trini's bright cloth up, she had dried the legs of his pants with a spell. Then, seeing his amazement, she had opened her hands to show him a flickering flame dancing on her palm.

Not much use, though, except for drying clothes in the rain and starting a cooking fire, Francis thought. Still, when he started his breathing ritual to focus his mind this time, it wasn't the thrill of oncoming battle that flared inside him.

It was the rage and awe he had felt when he had used his magic properly for the first time. He had seen August, that slimy mind fucker prick, and rage had taken over. Francis had raised both hands, flicked his wrists up and *whoosh*. August had been consumed in flames.

It had taken a full day's rest to recover from it, but it had been so, so worth it. To see that asshole's face melt after all he had done...

The feeling of vengeance, the rush of delivering justice swept over Francis. Without thinking, he moved his hands as he had done that day.

A flame erupted, the heat roasting his face and arms. It hovered over the water, flickering with impossible life. It flared, brightened, then shrank and dwindled to nothing as the power leached out of Francis, leaving him tired and spent.

His knees gave out this time, and he fell back to sit on his ass.

"Well, I'll be damned," he said. With surprise, he realized he had doubted what he had done that day during battle, wondered if maybe the mystics had tricked him, or made the fire seem bigger than it was.

He had just raised a flaming tower over water, with nothing to feed on but a thin branch and a scrap of shirt. It had felt *incredible.*

"Lucky I didn't try it in the field," he gasped, trying to catch his breath. He felt like he had run across the horse paddock at full sprint. Twice!

Francis staggered to his feet, realizing it was past lunch and he was damned hungry. Despite the tremor in his muscles, he could walk. He set off for home, and hopefully, a good feed and short lie down. It had, after all, been a very big day for him.

As he reached the road to Annie's, a familiar figure approached.

"Ye feeling ok there, lad?" Bette asked.

Francis nodded. "Never better," he said with a grin.

And what's he been up to? Bette wondered, unable to see past Francis's pale face and wobbling legs. *Oh well, none of my business I suppose.*

She had enough to worry about, what with her position as the leader of the Tahn guard, her regular training sessions with the men, and now, Polly.

Bette had to admit, Polly had surprised her. The girl might be flighty and all too obsessed with her looks, but she was a fast learner and not afraid to get her hands dirty.

I wonder how fast she'd be progressin' if she wasn't so eager to impress a certain wee lad, Bette thought with a smirk.

The whole town was buzzing about Danil and Polly's fling, not that either of them had tried to keep it a secret. *And not,* Bette had to admit, *that I've dissuaded her from sharin' the gossip.*

When Bette and Tansy had agreed to tutor Polly in the arts of fighting, it had come with the benefit of an inside glance into the girl's relationship. And every other aspect of her life—Polly wasn't one to let silence exist, quickly filling any lapses of conversation with chatter.

Bette thoroughly enjoyed it after spending so much time in the company of grumpy old men. *Most* rearick, in fact, were grumpy. "Right bastards, they are," Bette said aloud.

"Who's a bastard?" Polly asked, falling into step beside Bette.

"Och, I didn't see ye there, lass. Gave me a right scare, ye did."

Bette grinned at her as they swung left, passed through a little gate, and came to the training yard.

They were using Lewis's old horse yard for training. He'd already had it set up with a small, fenced off area now used for sparring, and in a bigger space, some old horse jumps that Bette had stripped down and reassembled as an obstacle course.

"What are we practicing today?" Polly asked.

"You tell me. Can ye walk straight yet?" Bette asked with a snort.

Polly giggled. The last training session she had come to had almost been cancelled after an all-night romp in bed that left her aching and barely able to walk.

"All healed up. I bribed Mathias with a few treats for his bird," Polly admitted.

"Ye wicked thing!" Bette said. "He's got his hands full with those twit soldiers."

"Nah, he's already finished with them. He said they were easy to fix, once he knew what they ate. I think he might have let it drag on a bit, though, just to fuck with them."

Polly pulled out a small purse and removed some pins. Sticking them in her mouth, she gathered her long tresses up on top of her head and began fastening it in place.

"Bloody fools. Who trains an army and doesn't teach them basic survival? Poisonous berries my ass. Their biggest problem is plain old stupid-headedness."

Bette waited patiently for Polly to finish. At least she had forgone the multi-layered dress this time, opting for tight pants that hugged her figure and a loose fitting blouse.

"Are ye sure ye can move in those?" Bette asked, pointing at Polly's bottom half. "It looks like yer about to bust outta the seams."

"They're my favorite pair," Polly protested. "And anyway, I don't think anyone's going to wait for me to change clothes before they attack."

"Aye, fair enough." Bette stretched out, and nodded as Polly jumped in to join her as soon as she was ready. "Though, I don't think they're likely ta wait for ye ta do yer hair, either."

"They'll just have to," Polly said with a grin. "But really, I thought about cutting it all off."

"What? All those pretty locks?" Bette asked in shock.

Polly's hair came down to her ass and curled in perfect ringlets at the bottom. Bette didn't care much for 'pretty' hair herself, preferring a messy, frizzy style that gave no fucks, but knew Polly put a lot of effort into keeping hers healthy and clean.

Polly shrugged. "I don't think I'll go back to selling the chance to yank on it. It'll be nice to do something different." Polly moved into a cat pose, tipping her head up to the sky. "Bitch, this feels good. I've been so tight the last few days."

"I don't think yer boyfriend will be complainin' about *that*," Bette teased.

"I make sure he doesn't have anything to complain about," Polly said primly, moving to stand, then lean forwards to touch her toes.

"And he knows where to stick it even though he can't see?" Bette asked.

Polly tsked. "It's not like any other man can see without a lamp on."

"Oh, aye." Bette wondered how to broach the question she really wanted to ask. Unsure how to proceed, she instead told Polly to start performing the stances she had been shown.

"Defensive… no, arm a bit up there. Aye. Now, step in to attack… no, not like that. Ye need ta go low, like this." Bette demonstrated and Polly copied her perfectly. "Ah, ye got it!"

"How about you and Garrett?" Polly asked in between instructions.

"What about us?" Bette asked, cheeks heating up.

"Have you *gone low* with him yet?" Polly waited for Bette to respond, but saw she was struggling. "You don't know how to move things forward, do you?"

Bette shrugged. "Not a damn clue. It's like he's afraid of me, and I don't want the wee thing ta lose his breakfast if I go and say the wrong thing, ye know?"

"Ah." Polly walked over to pick up a blunt spear, then turned, ready for their sparring session. "Then, you need to make it seem like his idea."

"And how would I do that?" Bette asked, before thrusting her wooden sword forwards.

Polly spun out of the way, easily dodging the attack. "Get him a bit drunk—not too much, mind, or he won't remember the next day. Cuddle up to him and drop a vague reference to being sore. When he offers to rub your shoulders, say something cheeky."

Bette frowned, then swung the training weapon around her head. As she brought it towards Polly's shoulder, she asked, "Like what?"

Polly blocked the strike. "Something like—" she grunted, then shoved Bette's sword off "—You can massage it with your cock, if you want. He'll snort and blush, and then you act all shocked, like he just agreed."

"He'd go bury himself under a rock if I tried that!" Bette protested, moving back for another strike.

"Not if you keep it light. And kiss him before he has the chance to run." Rather than wait for Bette to attack, Polly tried to slip in, aiming the spear for Bette's chest.

The rearick slapped the spear away easily. "Are ye sure?" she asked, dubiously.

"What's the worst that can happen?" Polly asked. She stepped back when Bette came running at her. Bette jumped, brought the practice sword down across Polly's spear and barreled the girl to the ground.

"I could break him," Bette said with a wicked grin. "But that doesn't need to be a bad thing, aye?"

Polly puffed and gasped, trying to catch her breath as Bette untangled herself and stood.

"Yer not wearing armor under there, are ye?" Bette asked curiously.

In response, Polly rolled up her shirt. A sturdy corset covered her torso. "Nothing I wouldn't wear on a normal day," she explained.

"Let me guess, they're not goin' ta stop and let ye strip yer underclothes off before they attack?" Bette chuckled.

"If they did, they probably wouldn't go through with it," Polly said, swaying her hips. "I'd convince them to step down, let everyone go, and buy me a drink before they retreat."

Bette thought this was hilarious, bursting into laughter.

"That's enough fer today, I think," Bette said when she caught her breath. "Yer learnin', that's for sure. We'll turn ye into a fighter in no time."

"Really?" Polly's eyes lit up. "I mean, you did just slam me to the ground without even thinking about it."

"Aye, I did, but I'm a professional. I can't move as fast as ye do, but yer not as strong as I am. We'll teach ye to use that ta yer advantage. That, and yer hip-wigglin' distractions will get ye by in a pinch."

"Thank you, Bette," Polly said, all trace of humor gone. "I mean it. I never thought I could be anything but what I was. You've shown me that's not true, and I can't tell you what that means."

"Oh, aye," Bette said, uncomfortable with the show of gratitude. "It was nothin'."

CHAPTER TWENTY-SIX

Danil wandered through the barn, Mathias beside him. Through the druid's eyes, he saw the neat beds and tidy stacks of gear sitting on the clean-swept floor.

"Seems they're settling in," Danil commented. The soldiers hadn't even been in Tahn for a full day, and they had managed to set up the temporary shelter like an army barracks.

"In some ways, they are," Mathias replied non-committally.

Danil paused, using his magic to make sure no one was nearby. "What do you mean?"

Mathias sighed. "It's not a big town. You've got the barely-recovered local residents already under strain from a sudden influx of refugees. Now? A highly trained militia has been thrown into the mix."

"A highly trained militia who is only here under our word," Danil pointed out. "There aren't enough of them to fight back if they get themselves thrown out. Surely, they realize that?"

Mathias laughed. "Oh, they realize. And for a couple, they feel the shame of that, alongside the embarrassment of every local here knowing how they got sick. Bear's Grape is a pretty well-known bush to anyone who's spent more than a day outside."

"Ah." Danil started pacing again. "Even the nicest of people can be dicks when ego is involved."

"Yes, your relationship with Polly would attest to that." Mathias ducked as Danil threw a mock punch.

Danil knew gossip about his initial argument with Polly had filtered through the town, though he had since heard a few embellishments that were not true. He did *not*, for example, ogle her with moonstruck eyes. He couldn't even see!

"No one is going to let me live that down, are they?" Danil asked. He had already given up trying to correct the gross inaccuracies in the story.

"Nope," Mathias agreed.

"Well, then. I suppose we had better sort this little problem out before it turns into a big one." Danil headed for the door, Mathias close behind.

The bright afternoon sun had dipped low and Mathias blinked, eyes watering as the glare blinded him after the dim barn. Briefly disconcerted by the effect on his borrowed vision, Danil walked straight into the door frame.

"Ah! Dammit!" he cursed and rubbed his face, hoping it wouldn't bruise. Wouldn't *that* give the local grapevine something to talk about.

"You ok?" Mathias said, trying to smother his laughter.

Danil muttered something obscene, then gave Mathias a false, shiny grin. "Fucking wonderful, I am."

They headed to the hall, where dinner was just being laid on the table. Stepping inside, the tension in the air was palpable. The normally busy, bustling space was subdued, with a clear huddle of men in one corner, surrounded by an empty space.

"Well, that won't do," Danil said, gesturing towards them with his chin. "Can't make friends if you don't mingle at parties."

"Are you sure that forcing them is a good idea?" Mathias asked. "Maybe we should just watch and wait for a little."

Seeing the benefit in that—mainly, that he could eat first and work later—Danil agreed. "Food, then," he said.

They pushed through the crowd of people, and Danil noticed there was a higher than normal number of Tahn villagers present tonight. *They probably want to get a look at the newcomers,* he thought.

His guess was on target, as he listened to the suspicious, yet curious thoughts of those around him. A couple of those he mind-read had been taught to shield.

Danil made a point to seek those out and suggest they continue to practice their mental defenses even when in the safety of Tahn. This was something they discussed in their lessons, as the more they used the skill, the faster they would progress.

Danil finally made it to the buffet table. He reached for a bread roll and a hand smacked his away.

"Did I teach you nothing while you were staying at my house?" Annie snapped.

Danil winced. Annie hadn't hosted the group dinner since the first night, and he hadn't seen her behind the long table.

"Sorry, Annie." He used a fork to spear the roll and put it on his plate.

"I trust you're well?" she asked, examining him closely.

He hoped there was no dirt on his face, and if there was, that she wouldn't lick her thumb and wipe it off like his mother did when he was a child. "Wonderful. I miss your generous hospitality, though."

"And we miss your bad manners and quick wit." She smiled to let him know she meant it.

"What brings you down this way?" he asked, curious. Annie didn't avoid town, exactly, but she made the trip infrequently enough that people tended to notice when she did.

Annie shrugged casually, but seeing through her eyes, Danil

noticed her glance at the back of the room where the cluster of soldiers lurked. "Just keeping my eye on things."

"We've checked them out, Annie." Danil kept his voice low. "We wouldn't have brought them back if we thought it meant trouble."

"They might be the cause of it, but it won't be them starting it. I know the boys that grew up here. Hot headed and too damn big for their britches," she said evenly. "And that right there is a recipe for trouble."

As he loaded the creamy potatoes and thick gravy onto his plate, a performer named Teek moved up next to him.

"Watch it," Teek snapped as someone jostled him.

"Sorry," came the reply. Danil recognized the one who had bumped Teek as one of the new soldiers.

"You should be," Teek grumbled. "Why don't you go lurk over there with your friends so you're out of the way?"

"You gonna make me?" the soldier growled, immediately on the defensive.

Danil whispered a word, casting a spell to drain away the frustration and anger that suddenly spiked around him.

"Don't act like you own this town, boy, because you don't," Annie snapped at Teek, her eyes blazing. "And you," she said, pointing at the other man, "should remember who took you in when you needed it and show some appreciation."

At her words, the tension rose again and Danil struggled to keep it down. There were too many people to work on, and the moods around him were changing too quickly.

"Back to your seat, Ketter," a voice behind them said. It was Arnold, and he spoke with the authority of someone who expected to be listened to.

Someone grew a pair overnight, Danil thought. He nodded his thanks to Arnold and maneuvered through the watching people to follow him.

Arnold saw Ketter back to his group, then came over to speak to Danil. "Sorry about that," he said. "They're not normally this… well."

"Yes, they are," Danil corrected him. "Come on, Arnold, I'm a mind-reader. I can tell when you're lying."

Arnold's face flushed bright red to the roots of his hair. "You have my apologies. I'll say this then: they're a rough bunch, but I do believe they can do good things, given a chance. I know it's hard to believe," he admitted. "But I know it's true."

Danil scanned Arnold's mind and realized it *was* true. Arnold truly believed that his men were good people deep down.

"Fair enough," Danil said. "He wasn't the instigator, anyway. But we *can't* let a fight break out. Not here, not with these people."

"I understand." Arnold ran one hand through his thinning hair. "I've already told them if I hear of anyone making trouble, they'll be out on their ear."

"Do you think it will help if I talk to them?" Danil asked.

Before Arnold could answer, Gerard came up to them, walking with a swagger and a mean twist to his mouth.

Gerard was one of the biggest men in Tahn, and one of the biggest drinkers, too. Danil could smell the booze on his breath and knew that even if he could dull the man's emotions a little, the effect would be unpredictable at best.

Julianne? Danil sent, feeling her nearby. *Hall, now. Bring Marcus, if he's with you.*

On our way, Julianne sent back. Danil caught the fleeting image of the cottage Lord George had taken for his own and knew she would be there in minutes.

"Can I help you, Gerard?" he asked coolly, hoping he would get the message and back down before making a fool of himself.

"Yeah, you can." Gerard threw a glance over his shoulder, and Danil saw a group of his friends watching. Mack, Jarv, and Carey were all in Gerard's guard troop.

So, this is a group project, Danil realized. *Damned if I'm going to let them off the hook if this goes bad.*

"I wanna—*we* wanna know if the jerk who attacked Sharne in her house is here." Gerard puffed out his chest, glaring at the group of soldiers. The effect was reduced when he swayed a little and had to shuffle a foot to keep his balance.

"And does Sharne want to know?" Danil asked, his voice hard.

Gerard scowled. "Not your business, mucker."

Nearby, someone gasped. The word mucker was reserved only for the New Dawn, an insult designed to cause offense.

Danil didn't have it in him to be offended. He could sense Gerard's anger and his fear that these men were here under false pretenses. He could touch his outrage at the idea that one of them had snuck into a fellow soldier's home—a *female* soldier, at that—and almost killed her.

And, Danil could see without even trying that by morning, Gerard would remember none of this. He would be left with a headache and a sick stomach and, if he was lucky, a fuzzy recollection of all the booze he had drunk.

I'm here. Julianne's thought echoed in Danil's mind, and he felt a spike of fear. Despite his confidence that it was the piss talking, not the man, he knew a wrong move could spark a fight.

Stay outside, for now. If this explodes, you don't want the shit to splatter on you. Danil knew that if this went badly, Julianne's authority would have to remain untainted to sort it all out in the morning.

I'm sending Marcus in, she replied. *He won't knock any heads until you tell him to.*

Danil knew Marcus would hold to that, and his anxiety eased a little. Gerard, however, was getting impatient.

"You covering for our little criminal, mystic?" he growled.

At least he hadn't called him a mucker again.

"He's not here," Arnold said, hurrying up to stand beside

Danil. "I know who you're talking about, and we lost him. Dead, or defected. Not sure which."

"How do we know that's the truth?" Gerard asked, leaning forwards. "And if you know what he did, does that mean you were with him?"

They had never substantiated the rumor of a second intruder and Danil had hoped they never would. *He* knew it was Arnold and clenched his jaw, hoping the new commander would have the brains to stay quiet.

"Yes, I was," Arnold said.

Danil groaned internally. Of all the stupid things to say.

"My sergeant directed me to sneak into the town and steal food for our men. They were starving. As a soldier, I was trained to do as I was told, no matter how distasteful... so, I did it. We snuck around the wall, to the east." Arnold looked around, noticing the entire room had their attention on him.

"And then?" Gerard pressed.

"And then, we split up. I went for a farmhouse, figuring I could take back some eggs and maybe raid the cellar if it was outdoors. No, I'm not proud of stealing from hardworking folks," he added. "You have my deepest apology for that."

"But you didn't actually take anything, did you?" Danil asked, loud enough for those watching to hear.

Arnold shook his head. "There was a clatter, and yelling, so I ran. I made it back to camp before Sergeant Larson. When he came in, he was limping. He had been stabbed in the leg."

Danil felt Gerard's rage build, fueled by Arnold's story and the alcohol flooding his veins. Remembering something Artemis had said about the effect of magic on physiology, Danil cast a small spell.

It wasn't much, just enough to make Gerard's vision tilt a little to the side.

"Just like a coward," Gerard panted. He leaned to one side,

trying to compensate for his crooked eyes. "Blame… blame the…" he swallowed.

Danil tilted his sight back the other way and Gerard swayed. Then, the angry pink in his cheeks turned green.

Danil shoved Arnold, and he stumbled to the side. Just in time, too. A flood of frothy vomit shot from Gerard's mouth, right where Arnold had stood barely a moment before.

Everyone moved back, even those well out of range, as Gerard hurled again, the sound of choking gags eliciting some sympathetically green faces amongst the onlookers.

Even Danil had to press a hand to his mouth. He scurried back, using his magic to block out the smell.

"Oh, Bastard's oath, Gerard!" Mack yelled from behind. "Go on. Drag him outside."

Mack and Jarv grabbed an arm each, lifting the still-puking man off his feet and carrying him out, leaving a trail of slippery, foaming slop on the floor as they went.

"Sorry," Gerard gasped as they hauled him away. "That came outta nowhere."

Danil looked at the shocked faces around him and sighed. "Guess I'll be stuck cleaning up the mess," he muttered.

Arnold walked over to him, carefully skirting the puddle on the floor. "Show me where a mop is, friend, and I'll take care of it. My men will have this place spotless before you know it."

"We will?" one of them asked. "Come on, Sarge. You know I'm a sympathetic spewer."

He did look a little green around the gills. Danil waited to see what Arnold's response would be.

"Look, it's not pleasant, but you lot were asking for that. Throwing your weight around and snapping at people like they owe you a hot lunch." Arnold paused, letting them shuffle uncomfortably for a moment. "We did wrong to these people, and they took us in anyway. We're damned well gonna stay here until we pay that debt."

"Yes, sir!" The cry was a little weak, but Arnold straightened his shoulders, looking proud of them.

"I think," Danil said quietly, "You just became the leader they need."

Arnold blushed, then started barking orders for his men to find buckets, water, mops, and towels.

CHAPTER TWENTY-SEVEN

Looks like you have it under control, Julianne sent to Danil. The words were suffused with pride.

He skimmed her mind and found her waiting outside. He squeezed through the people to go to her, smiling as the villagers around him shouted offers to help the soldiers clean up Gerard's mess.

Danil pushed open the hall doors, sucking in a deep breath of fresh air. He almost choked on it as the acrid smell of vomit and the sound of retching reached him.

"Over this way!" Julianne called.

Danil hurried over, and they escaped around the corner.

"I never knew a man could hold that much booze," Danil commented once they were safely away. "It started coming and it just didn't stop!"

"Yes," Julianne said dryly. "Can't say I'm sad to have missed that particular demonstration."

"Sorry to drag you away from whatever you were doing," Danil said. "I really thought things were going to get ugly in there."

"You don't call *that* ugly?" she asked, jabbed her thumb over her shoulder towards what was now a quiet groan.

"I call it better than the alternative," Danil said. "And anyway, I didn't know the spell would *work*."

"Wait," Julianne's said, grabbing his arm. "You're saying you *made* him sick?"

Danil shrugged. "Yeah. I mean, he was right on the edge, so it's not like I caused it out of nowhere."

Julianne raised her eyes and gestured for him to explain.

"He was drunk—really drunk. And when he started going toe to toe with the soldiers we brought in last night, it looked like it was going to erupt. I tried leaching his emotions, but the alcohol was messing with the magic. So... I made the world a little crooked."

"You changed his vision and it made him puke?" Julianne asked skeptically.

"You've never been vomiting drunk, have you?" Danil asked. "When you're that sloshed, it doesn't take much to tip you over the edge. Convincing his eyes that everything was slanted a little to the left, while his body could feel that it wasn't..."

"Wow." Julianne grinned. "Guess you *can* teach an old dog new tricks."

Danil started to nod, then cried out, "Hey! I'm not old!"

She shoved him gently. "You're getting wiser. That means you're getting old."

"Well, in that case, you're *ancient*." Danil shoved her back, and she stumbled, laughing.

"Steady on. We still have work to do." Julianne sobered, and when Danil reached into her mind, he found it cluttered with everything she was taking care of.

"What can I do?" he asked, unable to untangle the mess of thoughts. He knew it was just her way of thinking—Julianne would be able to make perfect sense of that jumble.

"Lord George is ready to meet the soldiers. We haven't told

them about him yet, or about Ade. We wanted to make sure it was safe." Julianne's gaze focused on something in the distance. "I'll need you to work on them, make sure they're ready to fight at our sides."

"How long until this all blows up?" Danil asked, referring to the imminent attack from Rogan and the army of Muir.

Julianne shook her head. "No telling. Annie says something is in the air, though."

"So that's why she came down," Danil said.

"More or less." Julianne stifled a yawn behind her hand. "I'll get George. Can you let me know when this is cleaned up?"

"I will. Try to get an early night, though, ok?" he said as she moved away. "Don't want you sleeping through the battle with Rogan."

"Oh, don't you worry," she said with a fierce grin. "I'm looking forward to that far too much to miss it."

Danil watched her go, unwilling to return to the crowded hall until he heard buckets of water being sloshed out the door. Once he was sure the smell had mostly gone, he returned.

He was gratified to see Gerard sitting on a stool, back against the wall as Mack fanned his face.

Mack looked up and gave the mystic a respectful, but slightly apologetic nod. Danil returned the gesture and went over to speak to Arnold, who was supervising the last of the cleanup.

"Still smells like shit," Danil commented.

"That it does," Arnold said. "But damned if it hasn't seemed to sort things out better than a dust up in a brothel."

"I... wouldn't know what you mean," Danil said, faltering.

"Oh? You've never taken a squad out for a night of relaxation?" At Danil's confused look, Arnold explained. "When two lads get their eye set on the one girl, whoever she doesn't choose gets his dick in a knot."

Trying not to visualize that, Danil nodded.

"So," Arnold explained, "You let them fight it out. Winner gets to buy the loser his next round with the girls and walks away with the respect of the men. Establishes the pecking order and makes sure there are no hard feelings the next day."

"Ah… yeah, I still don't get it," Danil admitted.

Arnold shrugged, grinning. "You'd have to be there."

Francis walked past, his arms loaded with bunches of lavender. He set about stripping the small, purple flowers into a collection of china plates and metal baking dishes.

A girl stood over him, telling Francis when each container had enough in it, and where to put them around the hall.

"You ready, Frank?" she asked. Casually, she raised her hands and a small flame flickered, then jumped from one to the other.

Francis shook his head as she juggled the fire. "Trini, has anyone told you you're a showoff?"

"Ha. I'm not the one who lit a whole pond full of water alight." She threw the tiny fire at him and he flinched, but it disappeared before touching him. "I'll have you dancing in the flames in no time, you'll see. First, we gotta get rid of this smell."

Trini walked around the room, small columns of smoke erupting from the dishes and pots as she passed them. The scent of smoky lavender rose to freshen the air.

"Oh, that's better," Danil said, relieved.

He and Arnold watched as Francis squatted by one of the pots, his hand hovering over it. He closed his eyes and screwed up his face.

"You're heating some leaves, not taking a shit," Trini taunted from across the room.

Francis's eyes snapped open. He opened his mouth to respond, then closed it, shuffling around the pot to turn his back on her. He blew out a hard breath, lifted his hand again, and stared.

A moment later, his eyes turned black and a sliver of smoke rose from the flowers.

Danil raised one hand in a silent fist pump. He waited until the smoke dissipated and Francis's eyes cleared before letting out a holler.

"You did it! You're a Bitch-damned physical mage!" Danil went over to clap him on the shoulder.

Francis blushed. "Yeah. I guess so." A grin spread over his face as it sank in. "Yeah. Yeah! I'm a magician!"

"We'll celebrate tomorrow," Trini said, darting over to give Francis a hug. "I'll show you what you'll be able to do after a bit of practice."

He awkwardly gave her a quick squeeze before stepping out of her embrace. "I don't think I'll ever be as good as you," he said.

"Nonsense," Danil said. "You'll start to progress faster now that you have a real teacher."

"Bastian did ok," Francis said, grimacing. "We only burnt down half a building between us."

At the smattering of laughter, Francis relaxed.

"Good work, lad. Good work," a bellowing voice called from the doorway. Lord George stepped inside, beaming. "Young Trini said she'd been working with you—hope you didn't pick up any of her bad habits."

"Me? Bad habits?" she said in mock outrage. "I'm a pillar of decency."

"Ha. You don't fool me, girl," George said with a fatherly smile. "But you did well with this young man. Who knows, maybe you'll train him up enough to serve with my personal guard."

At the mention of his guard, George's eyes flicked to Arnold and the rest of his men. They stood, dumbstruck, staring at the Muir lord with pale faces.

"You're... here?" Arnold gasped.

"I am. And, speaking of my guard..." Lord George scanned their faces. "They seem to be under the sway of Rogan, the cunning bastard. I'm in need of a trained force, one led by a good man who is willing to pledge allegiance to me."

Arnold dropped to one knee. "My Lord. I pledged to your son; we all did. We failed him. We would all give our lives to rectify that."

George walked over and looked down at Arnold. "*He* failed *you*. Perhaps, I failed you, too."

"You were up against a force you couldn't defend against," Danil pointed out. "I wouldn't exactly call that a failure."

"Still, my son would have led his men to disaster eventually." Lord George sighed when Arnold dropped his eyes guiltily. "Don't be ashamed for thinking the same thing. I know he was an idiot, but I was just too damn weak to do what I should have."

"Lord George the Third was an honorable fighter," Arnold said after a moment's pause.

"Diplomacy is never unwelcome," Lord George said with a smile. "But there's really nothing else you could say about him that isn't an insult."

"My lord… if there is any chance you'd take us on…" Arnold faltered, falling silent.

"Was I too subtle? I expect it. You'll serve as my personal guard as a temporary measure. Once Rogan is ousted and we sort out who is left, you will integrate with my existing guard." George lifted his head a little. "Will you and your men swear to me?"

Arnold sucked down a shaky breath. He didn't speak for a moment, but the moisture glittering in his eyes gave those watching confidence in his answer.

As one, the soldiers standing behind Arnold knelt, heads bowed.

"We will, my lord. Life and soul."

"Life and soul," echoed the others.

"I accept your pledges." Lord George patted Arnold on the shoulder and motioned for him to rise. "Your first order is to go and get some sleep. When Rogan attacks—and we believe that will be soon—you will fight alongside the soldiers of Tahn."

"Yes, my lord." Arnold's voice still trembled with emotion.

George gripped his shoulder, looking into his eyes. "You will be fighting men you have served alongside. Our aim is not to kill them—but if we have to in order to remove Rogan from power, we will."

Arnold swallowed. "Yes, my lord." He spoke softly, this time.

"Life and soul!" the men behind him cried out, and Arnold let out a choked laugh. "Life and soul!" he echoed. "For Muir! Life and Soul!"

CHAPTER TWENTY-EIGHT

Rogan tapped his fingers on the arm of the chair. The room was empty, silent except for the *tap, tap, tap* of his fingernail on hardwood.

"How shall we celebrate our victory, Julianne?" Rogan asked.

He cocked his head, listening.

"Really? I don't like that idea at all. I'd much rather a small, intimate event. Just the three of us."

He paused again, then said, "Why, Adeline, of course. If not for her, we wouldn't be here today."

After another short silence, Rogan opened his mouth to speak again, but was interrupted.

"Lord George, the soldiers are ready to move out on your command." The weedy young man stopped talking, suddenly worried by the dark look in his master's eyes.

"Hasn't anyone taught you not to speak over others?" Rogan said.

"No one was speak—" the boy said, then stepped back. "Your voice. It's different."

Rogan cursed. He'd worn Lord George's image for so long it

was second nature, but disguising his voice was distasteful. He had forgotten to deactivate the spell before answering.

"Lord George?"

Rogan whispered a word.

"Lord… Lor—" the boy stepped inside the room, then fell to his knees. Tears sprang from his eyes. "No. Please, no." He belted his face against the floor. "No! Help me!"

He smashed his face again, pounding it on the hard stone, over and over. His cries were soon stifled by the blood choking him as he destroyed his skull, only stopping the rhythmic destruction when he finally collapsed.

Rogan stood. "My dear, I apologize for the display. It was… necessary."

He nudged the body with his toe, unsure if the boy was dead or merely unconscious. A quick brush with his mind magic revealed him to be alive.

"Ugh. How distasteful." Unable to use mental magic on a comatose body, Rogan debated finishing the job manually. The blood pooling on the floor touched his shoe and he stepped back.

"Drown, for all I care," he muttered. Bodies were such a bother. They tended to upset people, though Rogan wasn't entirely sure why. He would have to brainwash people to ignore this, and have someone take care of the cleanup.

"Perhaps I'll leave it until I get back." Satisfied with the choice, Rogan swept out of the room, pulling the heavy doors closed behind him. "Come, Julianne. Let us go and crush the city of Tahn."

The hallways of the lord's manor were quiet. Most of the staff were busy, madly preparing to send off the army. It was the first real battle Muir had experienced, apart from a few skirmishes with neighboring regions over the resources in the area.

Why fight over hogs and trees when you can let someone else do the work, then hand them over? Rogan wondered. *No wonder these fools have such miserable lives.*

He shoved at the doors of the manor, shielding his face from the bright morning sun. The street outside was busy, cluttered with people and horses. Cries went out as Rogan, still under the spell making him look like Lord George, was recognized.

"Our mighty leader is here! To battle! Life and soul!"

Rogan basked in the adoration, his smile beaming out as he walked among them. One man led a horse up to him, a pure black stallion with a spirited gait. Rogan pulled himself on the horse's back, then raised a hand for silence.

"My people!" he began, waiting for the fresh cries to die down before continuing. "People of Muir! You have my humble thanks. The sadness and grief at my daughter's kidnapping, the worry I feel for her... Gone!"

Cheers rose up again, this time bringing a prick of irritation. He had, after all, just killed a man for interrupting his conversation.

"My friends, our mission is clear. We will take no prisoners, show no mercy. Today, we shall prevail. Today, we ride for Adeline!"

This time, he gestured with his hands, and the yells and cheers reached a deafening crescendo. He rose to stand in his stirrups, pumping his fists, sending out wave after wave of magic to imbue the crowd with excitement and bloodlust.

He knew it wouldn't last. They had a day and a half's ride ahead, but it would let them leave Muir hearing the cheers of the townspeople they left behind. Not that there were many—Rogan guessed that almost everyone in the town with a horse had turned out to ride with him to Tahn.

"To Tahn!" he called out and kicked his horse.

The horse shied. The people clogging the streets blocked the way and were too stupid to move. Growling, then yelling, Rogan tried to get them to move, but the cacophony of excited men and women drowned out his words.

Finally, Rogan send a blast of magic to the biggest man, on the biggest horse he could find. His target yanked the reins in his hand, making his horse rear up with a whinny. He bolted, forcing a path through the press of riders.

Rogan followed, face set in a snarl. *Insolent fucking whelps. They ruined my speech.*

He didn't look back to see if they followed. He could hear his generals, mostly new hires with few brains and even less experience. They yelled instructions and insults, but it did the job.

The thump of hoofbeats soon increased and before long, Rogan flew down the road following by a line of riders racing to keep up.

We're coming for you, my pet, he thought. *You'll be so happy to see me.*

CHAPTER TWENTY-NINE

Julianne walked quickly, clutching the small note in her hand. "They're leaving—no, they *left*, early this morning," she explained.

Bette let out a low whistle. "Well, it doesn't matter *when* they come; we could always be readier. But, we'll do."

"Do you think you can get the new men integrated by morning?" Marcus asked.

Bette had spent the afternoon speaking with the new soldiers, along with the troops she, Garrett, and Marcus had recruited in Tahn. A few volunteers from Madam Seher's theatre had joined them, too.

"They're still a wee bit wary of the situation, but this news will change that. Nothing like the prospect of a knife in yer guts to get ye ta co-operate with the man fightin' beside ye." She clicked her tongue, thinking. "Training might be a mistake. We don't want ta be caught with our pants down."

"I agree. Perhaps you should roster half of them on watch and give our men a chance to work with them in small groups?" Marcus suggested.

"Aye. Do ye think they'll make it here by mornin'?" Bette asked.

Julianne shook her head. "From the sounds of it, he would be bringing half the city. They have supply wagons, a weapons cache… everything but a medical tent."

"That says a lot about 'is motives," Bette commented. "He doesn't care how many men he loses. Crazy bastard."

"Crazy, but be prepared for a siege, by the sound of it," Marcus said. "He has to know using Muirians as cannon fodder won't sit well with any of us, especially George and Adeline."

"Yes," Julianne agreed, "but he's whipped them into a frenzy. They think we killed George and kidnapped Adeline."

"So?" Marcus said casually. "We can just throw them on the lookout tower. Once the army sees them, they'll back down."

Julianne shook her head. "He's an illusionist, remember? Anything he sees us do, he can use to his advantage. We'll need to be smarter than that."

Marcus sighed. "Whatever happened to a good old-fashioned sword fight?"

Bette nodded in sympathy. "If ye don't want 'em runnin' inta our pointy sticks, ye'd best have a plan before they get here."

"Before they get here?" Julianne laughed. "Bette, I've had a plan since the day Adeline stepped foot in Tahn."

"Of course, ye bloody did, ye smartass." Bette shook her head. "Serves me right for doubtin' ye."

"I'm surprised she even needs us around," Marcus said. "In fact, if we weren't here, Jules would probably have already won the battle, freed both towns, and tied everything up in a neat little bow."

Julianne shrugged. "Maybe. But then, who would get up at three in the morning to make me a cup of tea because I'm too busy to sleep?"

Marcus sighed. "I'm the tea-lady. The fucking *tea-lady!*"

"And so good at it, too," Julianne said, leaning over to kiss him on the cheek. "But now, I need you to go be someone else's tea-lady. I have to go see someone."

She veered off to the left, leaving Marcus to mutter at Bette about how unappreciated his tea-brewing skills were.

She found Artemis in his room, scribbling formulas on a scrap of paper.

"If they see him die... well, that's easy enough. He won't be that stupid, though, surely? Any number of things could... but if it relies on his connection. No getting around that, not unless he stays alive. Hrmm. Perhaps the answer, then, will lie in the solution."

When Julianne's shadow darkened his doorway, he ignored it. When she knocked, he spat. "Go away. I'm busy."

"You're always busy," Julianne said. She walked in, completely uninvited, and parked herself in the way of the small lantern.

Artemis slammed his pencil on the table. "And *how* do you expect me to fulfil your request when I'm plagued by interruptions? At least *seven times* in the last hour!"

"Artemis, you've had someone visit twice today. You didn't notice either time, the food Tessa brought is still sitting at the door." Julianne reached into her pocket and pulled out a bread roll.

Artemis's nose twitched as the aroma of warm bread filled the room. A rumbling growl from his stomach silenced the protest coming from his mouth. "Still. I've been interrupted this week. I think. At *least* once!"

The bread was soft and fresh enough that the butter inside hadn't quite melted. He shoved it in his mouth, taking the largest bite that would fit.

"A bird came," Julianne said, face somber. "We're out of time, Artemis."

"And?" he snapped, words muffled by the mouthful of food. "I told you, I can't give you an anthwer until we know what eggthactly he thaid..." he swallowed with a hard gulp. "Said, to form the death spell. One little word could change everything, for better or worse."

Julianne sighed. "Well, then, we'll just have to keep him alive until we figure it out."

"And you'll leave me alone until then?" Artemis asked hopefully.

He stuffed the last bite of bread between his lips and Julianne realized he had eaten it in two bites.

"Not a chance," she said with a smile. "I need to ask you if the brainwashing spell you taught me is sound. I can't practice it on anyone, but I need to know—will it work when I need it to?"

"Well, it worked for *him*, didn't it?" Artemis mumbled. The fact that he had taught Rogan the spell was still a sore point to the old mystic. He sighed. "I never used it. It was never *meant* to be used! But *he* did, so he must have found a way."

"But, we can't know if he used it as you taught it, or if he altered it in some way," Julianne clarified. Sometimes Artemis's thought processes were perfectly on point. That was rare, though, and she had to know.

He nodded. "That's right." He looked away. "You'll... hold to your promise?"

She nodded. "I swear, Artemis. No one will ever learn this spell from me."

He nodded and turned away, sniffing and wiping his nose on the back of his sleeve. "I never meant for this to happen."

"I know." Julianne reached out to touch his shoulder. "We all know. And, we know you'll do what you can to fix it. For Tahn."

Artemis didn't turn back to her. He stared at the wall, silent.

She worried his silence meant he wouldn't fight, but she eventually felt his shields drop, just a little. She couldn't see into his mind, but she could sense his emotions.

He might be too proud to admit it, but Artemis was scared. Terrified, in fact. And yet, a thread of resolve ran through the fear, knitting it up in a tight bond. The fear would fuel him—fear of having to face this again, and fear of letting Tahn suffer from his mistake.

He would fight. No matter what, Artemis would stand with them in the battle for Tahn and Muir. He would lend his magic—and perhaps, his fists—to undoing the threat he had inadvertently created.

"Thank you, Artemis." Julianne stood and walked to the door. "When I get back to the Temple, I'll make sure your work is not forgotten."

That elicited a wave of teary gratitude from the old hermit. Though not all the magic he had discovered was safe to share, many of the techniques he had developed would move mental magic into the future.

The very existence of shared shields opened up new possibilities, and the formula he had come up with to reverse and heal the effects of the brainwashing spell would need to be recorded.

Artemis was driven by knowledge. He didn't care if he, personally, was remembered. In fact, Julianne had the feeling he would rather be forgotten. His research, however, was another story.

"Thank you," a soft voice called as she closed the door. Smiling, Julianne left him to his notes.

CHAPTER THIRTY

The next day was spent in quiet busyness. The people of Tahn—both residents and refugees—scurried around, stockpiling food in cellars in case of a siege, ripping spare sheets into bandages, and hurriedly reinforcing what little weapons and armor they had.

"Do ye think we have enough spears?" Bette asked after she returned from a quick bite of lunch.

"What?" Garrett asked. "Three for every man, and a hundred-twenty spare? Are ye serious?"

Bette shrugged. "By the time we throw a few in their faces, we might start runnin' low. Once the fightin' starts, ye can't exactly ask fer a time out ta restock."

Garrett shook his head. "I don't think ye'll be launching them from atop the wall. Julianne said we're to minimize the casualties."

Bette shook her head. "Does she know what happens in battle? We're not sittin' down to a tea-party. They'll be hammerin' in here tryin' to kill us!"

"Aye," Garrett said, quietly. "Because they think we stole their princess and want to raze their town. Can ye blame them for bein' a wee bit cranky with us?"

Bette sighed. "I suppose, under those circumstances…" She shook off her melancholy quickly. "If Julianne wants a non-lethal battle, that's what we'll do."

"Aye." Garrett straightened. "A spear-butt still causes a world of hurt, and a few holes in legs won't exactly be *fatal*, as long as we look after the ones we knock over."

"What do ye think she'll do with young Adeline and 'er father?" Bette asked. "I know she's got somethin' planned. I saw her sneakin' around with some cloaks earlier."

Garrett shrugged. "If she didn't tell us, it must be for a reason. Rogan must have a few muckers floatin' about, and if they get wind of her plan, it might just go badly."

Bette nodded in understanding. She resolved to think no more about what she had seen, and to ignore anything else she came across. "Right, then. Can ye take point here? I need ter go check the men on watch."

Garrett saluted and watched her leave. "Damn, she's a fine lass," he muttered.

He paced back and forth in the small watchtower, waiting for her to return. Running his gaze over the tree line and along the narrow road that led from Tahn to Muir, he wondered how long they had.

His bones itched for a fight, and his stomach quivered with nerves. He wasn't afraid of dying or getting hurt—this nervousness was new to him, though he had felt it last time they faced off with a Muir army.

He was afraid of letting Bette down. She had worked her ass off to train the men and women of Tahn, to sculpt them into fighters worthy of the spears they bore.

She was a good leader and, like all good leaders, those she led viewed her with respect and worked to make her proud.

Even Garrett. "Aye, a fine lass, and a fine commander, too."

He went about his business, checking the quality of the spears stored nearby and keeping a close eye on the tree line, until a cluster of voices from below caught his attention.

Lord George approached the watchtower alongside Marcus and Julianne, causing a few of the guards on watch to turn and greet them.

"Eyes front, lads," Garrett reminded them. "Lewis? Go find Bette; she's doin' the rounds."

Lewis jogged off as Garrett headed down the rickety steps to greet the lord of Muir.

"Ahh, Garrett." Lord George gave him a respectful nod. "Where is your commander?"

"Ye mean Bette?" They had never discussed titles, figuring their ragtag army would just sort out their own pecking order, with Bette at the top. "I sent one of the men to get her, so she'll be along shortly."

"On my way," Bette called, running over. "Is there news?"

George shook his head. "No, nothing like that. I've been speaking to Marcus and Julianne, though." He looked from one rearick to the other. "I know this isn't the time for it, but I may not get another chance. Bette, Garrett, what are your plans when this is over?"

Bette gave Garrett a glance, and he saw his own look of confusion mirrored on her face. "My lord, I haven't given it a thought. I wouldn't leave Tahn undefended, though, and I think I speak for all of us when I say we won't abandon the town if we're needed."

Lord George cleared his throat. "Julianne has a duty to the Temple she leads. Marcus has informed me he will follow her when she goes. However, I'd like to offer you both an invitation."

"Aye?" Garrett said, curious.

"Yes. Tahn has changed. I doubt these people will be able, or even willing to go back to their quiet life of farming once this is over." He paused, taking Bette's measure. "I've lost men. Tahn needs to be able to defend itself. Will you stay on as Captain of the Tahn force, with Garrett serving as your First Lieutenant?"

Bette's jaw dropped. "Sir... Lord George... I don't have the experience! I'm not trained, I barely—"

"Oh, shut yer bloody mouth, woman," Garrett said. "Ye've done more fer these men than any rearick troop leader I've seen. Ye've got the head and the skills for it, so don't sell yerself short."

Bette's eyes started to redden. They sparkled, but she bit down hard on her cheek to stem any rogue tears. "I would be honored," she said, voice husky.

"If Bette is staying, and if she'll take me as her first, ye have my pledge, too," Garrett said without hesitation.

"Thank you," George said. His shoulders dropped as a hidden tension left his body. "You have put my mind at ease. I know you'll both do well."

"Army sighted! They're coming!" The call rang along the narrow bridge running behind the wall.

Bette gave Lord George a quick salute, then snapped, "Thank ye, sir, but I gotta run."

"Go! Go, and defend our town!" George called.

"I'd best move along, too, sir," Marcus said, then dashed off.

"Well, Julianne. Should we get ready?" George said, turning to her.

"Tell Tess and Adeline. Get ready, but don't come out until I give the signal." She gave him a reassuring pat on the shoulder. "I have to join the others."

George watched her go, wishing he had her unwavering confidence. Still, it had infected him a little. As he went to find his daughter, he realized he could actually entertain the idea that they may just pull this off.

He picked up speed, walking as fast as he could to the small cottage that Julianne had insisted he stay in.

"Danil!" he called, seeing the blind mystic strolling past.

Danil smiled and opened his mouth to speak, then read what

was in George's mind. "Tessa is in the hall!" he called out, knowing George would look for her first.

He broke into a run, shutting off his sight gained via George's eyes and relying on his instincts to lead him to the watchtower. Though no one was around to lend him their sight, he arrived quickly and without getting lost or tripping.

His vision flared to life as he touched the minds of the people around him, using their eyes to see again. Spears were being handed out and leather armor strapped on.

"Artemis!" Danil called, spotting the old man hovering on the edges of the crowd.

Artemis hurried over, a deep frown etched on his face. "Danil? There are so many people. I can't work around this many people."

"It's ok. I'll take you somewhere safe." He looked around for Polly. "Tansy?" he called, seeing the performer slipping a brass-ringed corset on. "Where's Polly?"

Tansy jerked her head to the left and Danil grabbed Artemis's arm, pulling him along. He spotted her binding her hair back, a small, curved sword at her feet.

"I need you to come with me," he told her.

Polly's eyes flashed. "No. I'm going to fight. You can't stop me —Bette has been—"

"I know, she's been training you. That's why you need to come with me," Danil said. He grabbed her sword and gestured for her to hurry.

Polly started walking, her hands still busy in her hair. "What do you mean?" she asked, casting a longing glance over her shoulder.

"Bette said you're one of the few she'd trained in close fighting. We need a bodyguard—you're it." Danil pulled Artemis along the wall until he found what he was looking for. A cellar, the small door semi-hidden behind a building with small steps leading underground.

"Dammit, Danil, if you're just trying to keep me away from the action…" she said, the warning clear in her voice.

"Polly, I can't fight. I can take down a normal soldier, but if they bring a mystic with them, one who is shielded, I'm about as vulnerable as a canary in a cage. I don't think Artie here is exactly a hand-to-hand expert, either."

"So, we're going to hide out down here?" Polly asked dubiously.

"Artemis, Bastian, and I need to link our shields so we can prevent Rogan attacking us while we use our magic. Sharne is guarding Bastian at the other end of the wall. If we don't do this, George and Adeline will be completely vulnerable." He looked at her, beseeching.

"Stay near the back," she said, stepping up by the door with her sword drawn. "I'll make sure you aren't interrupted."

Danil grinned. "You ready, Artemis?"

The old man nodded nervously. Danil's eyes dimmed for a moment, then, like four glowing lights in the depths of a cave, Artemis and Danil's eyes lit as they cast the shielding spell.

"Never get used to that," Polly muttered. Neither man seemed to notice, so she made herself comfortable, sword in hand, and prepared herself for the watch.

CHAPTER THIRTY-ONE

Rogan's horse paced down the line as he watched the wall. Tahn soldiers scurried along, their heads barely showing as they bobbed along. *Since when does Tahn have soldiers?* he wondered.

Occasionally, one would stand, hand shielding the sun as they scanned the army waiting outside the woods. Each time, the waiting army rustled with nerves.

Rogan ran his eyes over his own men as they scrambled to set up tents and distribute rations. Bile burned in his throat.

Pathetic, he thought. *Weak, desperate men fighting for a woman who will never see them.*

He had scanned their minds, randomly dipping in and out of people's thoughts as they had travelled. All of them, focused on the mission ahead and marched to free their beloved Adeline.

He couldn't sense their lust, but he knew it was there. Men didn't admire a woman for anything else. The pride in her leadership and gratitude for the service she had paid to the poor and underprivileged was a cover, a story they told themselves to hide thoughts of fucking her, thoughts Rogan knew were there even if he couldn't find them.

They've lied so well, they've even convinced themselves. Unable to look at them without feeling ill, Rogan turned his attention back to Tahn.

"Fuck the tents," he growled. "Fuck the rations. You!" he called to a man standing on a wagon of carefully packaged food. "Destroy those. We won't be here long enough to need them."

"De—destroy them, my lord?" the man stammered.

Unwilling to expend the effort needed to repeat himself, Rogan muttered something else, instead. Immediately, the man turned, unlaced his pants and started to piss. He soaked the food, heedless of outraged cries from those watching.

"*DID YOU HEAR ME?*" Rogan roared to those complaining. "We fight at daybreak! If you don't take this city, you don't eat. Is that enough incentive for you?"

Back at Tahn, Julianne caught the exchange. It was a stretch to read minds at that distance, but the effort was worth it for that vital bit of information.

"He's going to attack at dawn," she said. "And he's starving the men until the battle is over. They'll be tired and weak by the time things start getting really hectic."

"Fool," Marcus muttered. "What is he thinking?"

Taking his question literally, Julianne shrugged. "His shield is too strong, he must have other mystics with him. I can only touch the minds of the fighters."

Lips quirking up in a smile, Marcus didn't explain it had been a rhetorical question. "He sounds volatile, Jules. I still think we should keep up the guard."

"Oh, absolutely. But it'll give me a chance to put my own plans into action before the swords start flying." She grinned, and turned to go. "I'll get the others and meet you back here."

"Wait!" Marcus grabbed her arm and kissed her deeply before she left.

"What was that for?" Julianne asked, touching a finger to her tingling lips.

Marcus laughed. "You're about to do something incredibly

dangerous—don't look at me like that; I know it's necessary. I just wanted to remind you why you need to come back in one piece."

Julianne socked him in the shoulder, and he winced. "Of course, I'm coming back. I promised Annie I'd bake pies with her once we're done here. She seems to think I can't cook, and is rather insistent on being the one to teach me."

"You'd come back for Annie, but not for me?" With a wounded look, Marcus gave her a gentle shove towards the ladder. "Go, get the others. I'll be waiting patiently as always."

"Good boy," Julianne said, giving him a quick wave before she disappeared down the ladder.

She set off for the cellar where Danil would be hiding, almost getting her head chopped off when she poked it in.

"Yikes! Sorry, Julianne. I didn't recognize you in the dark." Polly tucked her sword away.

"I need to take Danil here on a little mission. Although…" Julianne eyed the sword. "That blade of yours may come in handy. Wanna come?"

"Sure!" Polly grinned, glad for the chance to escape the dim little hole.

"Good riddance," Artemis snapped. "All these thoughts of naked men are driving me insane."

Julianne's jaw dropped.

"I told you, old man, if you don't wanna see what's in my head, then stay out!" Polly pulled at Danil's hand, helping him stand.

"I *am* out. You leak." Artemis settled back into his corner, seemingly content to stay there.

"I leak? That's disgusting!" Polly grimaced.

"He means your thoughts are strong and loud," Danil explained. "And he's right. Hell, Polly, the thoughts that go through your head when you're bored…"

Polly grinned. "Girl's gotta have something to occupy her mind. You really need to find a better word for it, though."

"Come on, you two," Julianne said, noticing the look of irritation on Artemis's face. "We'll need Bastian for this, then we have to find Adeline."

"What are we doing?" Polly asked as they hurried through town.

"We're making a preemptive strike," Julianne said cryptically. "Hopefully, one that will save a lot of lives."

They found Bastian tucked away on the second floor of an abandoned building next to the wall. He had set himself up with a thin mattress and a blanket, and full box of dried fruit, bread rolls, and jerky.

"Hey," he said defensively, when Danil pointed it out. "Man's gotta keep his strength up!"

"Well, you'll need to eat on the run," Julianne said. "We're taking Adeline out to see her friends."

"You're what?" Bastian asked, eyes bulging.

"I don't know what Rogan has planned, but I'll bet it rests on her," Julianne said. "He's convinced those fighting for him that we've kidnapped Ade and are holding her captive. If she can convince even a few of them otherwise..."

"They'll desert," Bastian finished for her. "But, Master... you'll be leading her right into the lion's den. Hell, she'll be tugging on his tail and tickling his nose if your plan goes how you want it to."

"We'll be careful," Julianne promised. "If it looks too dangerous, we'll abandon ship."

Bastian eyed his cache of food and sighed. He stood, stuffing a handful of jerky in his pocket.

Julianne turned, then did a double take, coming back to the food cache. "How much of that do you have?" she asked, rummaging through the box. She stuffed her pockets with jerky and fruit and gave some to Danil to hold, too.

"Hey, that's Jessop's best jerky!" Bastian cried.

"And I appreciate your kind donation," Julianne chuckled.

"Come on. We have to find Adeline, then meet Marcus at the wall."

Adeline was eating an early dinner with her father when they arrived at the cottage. "Julianne! Is everything alright?" Adeline asked, jumping up from the table.

"Yes, the army is setting up camp for the night, so we think things will stay quiet until daybreak," Julianne said. "But we'd like to borrow your daughter for a few hours, if that's ok, Lord George?"

"Which one?" Tessa asked, stepping into the room.

She wore one of Adeline's gowns and had her hair done up to match. Julianne clapped. "Tessa, you look perfect!"

Tessa had Adeline's slim build and dark hair. With her clothes and makeup done, she could almost pass for the lord's daughter, though she was older.

Tessa curtsied. "Thank you, ma'am."

"Where are we going?" Adeline asked, pushing her plate away and standing. "Do I need to bring the robe?"

Julianne almost said no, then nodded. "Actually, that's a good idea. It will help to reinforce the image we send later."

Adeline pulled a white robe—one of Julianne's—off a hook on the door and slipped it on. "Off we go, then," she said, a thread of nerves working its way through her words. "Goodbye, Father. Stay safe."

"Me? You're the one out after dark with an army at the doorstep," George said. He sent a wistful look their way. "And I'm sure you'll enjoy every minute. I don't know if I'm more worried or jealous."

"You'll have your turn later, my lord," Julianne said wryly.

George erupted into a laugh. "Very well. If I don't see you before the battle, stay safe and fight well."

"I wish my father had been like yours," Julianne said as they hurried through the now-dark streets. "I wasn't even allowed to visit the market on my own, let alone face six hundred men and a psychopathic magician."

"Six hundred?" Adeline gasped.

Julianne nodded. "Give or take. We're basing our estimates on inexperienced men's thoughts and a couple of *really* stupid birds."

Remembering her last encounter with a 'stupid bird', Adeline groaned. "If it's Percival, then it could be anywhere from fifty to five thousand," she said.

"Pretty much," Julianne agreed. She stepped back to let Adeline climb the ladder first. "When you get up top, stay low," she warned.

Julianne went next, Polly, Bastian, and Danil following. They crowded onto the platform alongside Marcus and Bette.

"Interesting choice of companions," Marcus remarked.

Marcus didn't look at Polly, but Julianne knew that's who he referred to. She could have slipped an explanation in his mind, but didn't, instead saying, "I only want the best."

Bette gave a satisfied snort and Polly's mouth twitched into a tiny smile.

"Alright, stop lollygaggin'," Bette said. "I didn't want anyone ta know of yer little jaunt across the field, so we've only got a wee bitta time before the next rotation comes along."

"Are we ready?" Julianne asked.

Danil and Batian's eyes cleared and Julianne whispered something under her breath. She felt the magic course through her and directed a tendril towards Bastian. Almost immediately, she accepted another from Danil, completing the circuit.

Their shield was up and secure. Julianne said another word, her face serene as she cast a second spell.

"We're good. Stay close together and try to keep quiet. We can move fast, as long as we're steady. Nothing sudden, please," she said.

"Och, lass! That's bloody amazing, it is!" Bette stood back, twisting her head back and forth.

Polly whispered to Danil, "What's that about?"

"I cast a spell to hide us," Julianne explained. She realized the girl hadn't often seen her using magic and would be less accustomed to her eyes glowing than Danil's, who used his almost constantly. "We are, for all practical intents and purposes, invisible."

Polly lifted a hand up, looking at it with a frown.

"Sorry," Julianne said. "It won't work on us. Anyone out there, though—" she pointed at the army, then the town. "—won't see us, even if we're right in front of them."

"Aye," Bette confirmed. "Yer just, *poof*! Gone!"

Julianne picked up a rope that was tied to the watchtower railing. She pulled it, hard, checking it was secure. "Let's go."

She stood on the edge of the wall and leaned back, using the rope to hold her. Then, she jumped. Rappelling to the ground, she stood back to let the next person down.

"Bette?" she called softly.

The rearick stuck her head over the edge, looking about. "Ye there? I can't see ye."

Julianne cupped a hand and a tiny, glowing butterfly rose up. It darted past Bette, who gasped in delight. "When we get back, I'll send one of these. Don't let anyone up if you don't see it."

"Aye," Bette said. "Good luck!"

Moments later, the six set off, heading right for the enemy's den.

CHAPTER THIRTY-TWO

They crossed the field quickly, Adeline's cloak flapping in the breeze.

You're Adeline's guard, Julianne sent to Marcus. *No matter what, get her back to Tahn safely.*

What about you? Marcus thought.

I have Polly.

Marcus didn't reply, figuring he should count his blessing that she had even brought a second fighter with them.

They approached the edge of the army with caution, slowing to a stop to gauge the situation.

"They've got the real soldiers on watch," Marcus said. "Those guys will be harder to mess with."

"Especially because about half have some kind of magical interference going on," Julianne said. "Can we sneak past and enter from the back?"

They crept around, sticking to the shadows and staying close enough to see the sprawling mess of people, but not so close that they would be easily noticed, even without Julianne's spell hiding them.

About halfway, Julianne jerked a hand up. Everyone froze. A

man stumbled towards them, cursing at the uneven ground and lack of moonlight. "Bloody fools errand, this is," he grumbled. "I'm not a fighter. I shouldn't even be here."

"That's a mental magician," she whispered.

She straightened and stepped forward, then leaned over to pull Polly's sword from her scabbard. Lifting a finger to her lips and cautioning them to silence, Julianne quietly stepped up behind the man as he undid his pants.

When he was done pissing, he stumbled around to face Julianne. The sword she held was an inch from his eye.

He stepped past it without blinking. Julianne smiled and handed Polly back her weapon. Once he was a short distance away, Julianne said, "Sorry. Just making sure the spell is working."

Bastian gave a nervous giggle. "Guess that means it is," he said.

"You thought it might not?" Polly asked, head twitching back and forth as she watched for danger.

Julianne shrugged. "Usually, it's fine. But with all these mystics running around with triple-layered shields, I didn't want to find out the hard way."

"Fair enough." Polly waited for Julianne and Marcus to move back into the lead.

They finally spotted a small group of men sleeping on the grass, separated by a short distance from the main group.

"Start there," Julianne said. "Adeline, are you ready?"

They walked over, staying quiet and waiting until a three-man patrol had passed by. Julianne whispered something. "I've taken off the disguise," she whispered. "Say your piece and leave them with this." She thrust a handful of jerky and fruit into Adeline's hand, then stepped back.

Adeline approached the nearest man, shaking him awake gently. She pressed a hand to his mouth when he jerked up, then released it slowly.

"Hush," she said quietly. "I can't be seen by the others."

"Who… Lady Adeline?" the man said, eyes wide in wonder. The distant bonfire reflected in his eyes as tears welled.

"Joseph, isn't it?" Adeline said. "I met you, once. Your daughter goes to my father's school. Her name is Jessie?"

"Yes." Joseph gulped down a quiet sob. "Yes, Jessie's my girl. But your father—"

"That creep is *not* my father," she hissed. "His name is Rogan. He's a magic user, a despicable man masquerading as Father and lying about me, too. Joseph, I wasn't kidnapped."

"What?" he asked, bewildered. "Why are you here, then?"

"I fled here to escape Rogan," she explained. "Father is here, too, safe inside the city walls. Jospeh, you *must* leave. Don't fight Tahn. The people there are innocent."

Joseph screwed up his face in confusion. "That makes no sense." He rubbed his face. "Wait… is this a dream? Maybe I'm imagining you."

Adeline glanced at Julianne in alarm. "No! Joseph, I'm as real as you are. Please, you have to listen to me!"

"Adeline, we have to move," Julianne whispered. The sound of men chatting to each other buzzed in the distance, coming closer.

"Take these. Remember what I said." Adeline shoved the small pile of food at Joseph and rejoined the others.

They snuck out, and Julianne cast the invisibility illusion on Adeline once they were out of sight.

"This is useless," Adeline said. "By morning, he'll think it's all a dream, and he won't pay any attention."

"That's why you left him food," Julianne said. "Rogan destroyed their rations. When they see that, they'll know something happened, and when they start talking, only to find they all had the same dream?" Julianne smiled. "Trust, Adeline. Trust your people."

When they approached the next group, Adeline woke three of the sleeping men. Though dazed and wary, they seemed to accept that she was real. "Save the food until morning," she said, handing them each a small portion.

"Of course, Lady Adeline," they murmured, gazing at her in awe. "But… if you want us to desert Lord Geor—Rogan's army, shouldn't we go now?"

She shook her head, falling back on the instructions Julianne had given her. "You'll be caught by his patrols. Wait until morning, when Rogan calls the attack. When his men go forward, run like hell."

A chorus of assent buoyed her heart, and she left them feeling more confident than when she had spoken to Joseph.

Julianne's plan will work, she told herself. *When the men who aren't sure see the others leave, they'll run, too.*

They managed to speak to six more groups of men, Adeline insisting that they do their best to spread the rumor of her safety and encourage other Muir civilians to flee when the attack was called in the morning.

To some, she gave more details—about Rogan's tricks, and her father's status—but twice, she was interrupted by a guard or patrol and had to cut the meeting short. Each time, she left a small handful of snacks to fill their stomachs.

"This is the last one," Julianne said. "It's getting dangerous." A scan of the army's minds had showed they were getting restless. Some of the people Adeline had spoken to were already telling their friends of her visit, and sharing the small bounty she had left as proof.

"So, I'd better make it a good one," Adeline said, nodding confidently.

She crept past two tents and then into a third. Waking the two men inside, she quickly told her story, now well-rehearsed.

"If Rogan is really pretending to be your father, how do we know who you really are?" one of them said, suspicion etched all over his face.

Adeline faltered. So far, they had taken her appearance at face value.

"I know," the second man said. "Who really snipped your father's buttons off before his presentation, back when you and George were children?"

Adeline blushed. "Really? Of all the things to ask, you chose that?" She glared at him a moment, then said, "It was me."

"Ha!" the first man said. "It wasn't! You're fake, just like you said your father is."

The second one, though, shook his head. "Nah, Harvey. She's telling the truth, alright. My aunt was working in the manor and said Miss Adeline here was caught with a big pair of scissors and a handful of buttons in her room the next week. No one ratted her out. If she was lying, she'd have blamed her brother."

"I was trying to replace them with ones I'd made," she admitted, chagrined. "I was too young and silly to know paper buttons wouldn't hold worth a damn. When I couldn't fix it, I hid the evidence and let George take the fall."

"That's our Ade, alright," the second man said. He dropped his head. "I'm sorry, my lady. We shouldn't have questioned—"

"No!" she snapped. "It's a lack of questioning that got us here. Has no one noticed my supposed father's change of personality? Has *no one* asked why?"

They exchanged glances. "Well, can't say we couldn't see something had changed. Only, every time someone had the chance to ask him, they came back all convinced it was definitely him."

"Part of the magic," she explained. "Look, I'm running out of time. Will you help tell the others? I've only gotten to a few men, but if I don't get back to Tahn, things could go very badly in the morning."

They nodded eagerly. "At your service, Lady Ade. Life and soul."

They saluted and she impulsively leaned over to hug each of

them. "Thank you. I know the people of Muir look up to me and my father, but honestly, *we're* the ones who are blessed."

She wiped away a tear and scurried away, safe under Julianne's spell once again.

"We've done what we can," Julianne said. "Hopefully, it's enough to disrupt the attack tomorrow. All I need is a chance—if I can get to Rogan, that bastard will go down."

Adeline nodded. "The more that flee, the less we'll have to worry about hurting innocent people."

"Do you really think we can pull this off, Jules?" Marcus asked.

She knew without asking that he was really asking a different question. He wanted to know if she could really sneak through an army, kill Rogan, and return in one piece.

"With one hand behind our backs," she said with a grin.

"Which begs the question," Polly said, "why you don't just sneak on in and kill him now?"

Julianne shook her head. "He's surrounded by a group of soldiers and mental magicians who are completely under his spell, and well-shielded to boot. If I try it now, then either they'll catch me, or Rogan will die by mistake."

"And that's a bad thing?" Polly asked, one eyebrow shooting up her forehead.

"If Rogan dies, his minions will go nuts and kill a bunch of people, then themselves," Danil explained. "War is messy and disorganized, especially when you're fighting with an untrained force. Much better chance of sneaking in, knocking him out, and buying enough time to dismantle the death spell."

Polly just stared. "Wow. This guy is a grade A villain, isn't he?"

The whole party nodded in unison.

"Well, good thing we're not gonna let him get away with it," she said. Polly pulled out her sword and gripped it. "Let's go. We've got a war to win."

CHAPTER THIRTY-THREE

Rogan stood high in his horse's stirrups, poking out over the swollen mass of men. Most were on foot—only his trained soldiers and loyal magicians were allowed horses.

The silence would have been unnerving to a lesser man. As Rogan eyed the woman atop the the wall, though, every fiber of his being was pulled to her.

"Julianne, we have you surrounded!" he called. "Surrender. Open your gates and give your people the chance to live."

"Fuck you, Rogan!" she called back.

He cursed her shields. It would be so much easier to communicate using their magic. "Now, dear, cursing is for the dregs of society. We're better than that, aren't we?"

"How is this for *better*? Order your men to stand down. Give yourself over to us. We'll make sure you get the help you so clearly need." Her frosted gaze gave no hint of the fear she must surely be feeling.

Rogan heaved a sigh, only now paying attention to the mutters of his men.

"Rogan? Who's Rogan?" Several eyes turned to him. Farther off, the murmurs held hints of resolve rather than confusion or surprise. "Kev was right!" And "...telling the truth?" reached his ears, but he brushed them off.

"We know you have Adeline, the Lady of Tahn. And I—Lord George, her father—" Rogan looked around as if to reassure his men that he was speaking the truth. "I demand you turn her over, safe and unharmed."

A second figure stepped up next to Julianne and Rogan's heart jumped into his throat. Two women, one in shining white and the other wearing vibrant blue, stood tall and proud.

"I am not a prisoner!" Adeline called.

Rogan smiled, a bubble of laughter rising in his chest. *Damn fools! They walked right into my trap.*

He whispered a few words and for the briefest moment, those watching felt a flicker in their vision, like a distant wave of heat rising up to distort the image of the women standing above them.

Buzzing filled their ears and drowned out speech as the white-robed figure raised a hand. A dagger sparkled in the morning sun for a moment as time seemed to freeze. It plunged towards the woman in blue, stabbing into her back.

She fell, crumpling, then tumbling backwards off the wall as Julianne turned her glare to the army.

Breathing hard and flushed with excitement, Rogan released the spell. "Now who's in charge, bitch?" he panted.

Julianne ripped off her cloak. Rogan started, squinting for a better look. *How?*

"I am Adeline, and this is my father!" She shook out her long, dark hair as the illusion fell away. Lord George—the *real* Lord George—stepped up beside her.

"That man is an imposter!" George yelled, thrusting a finger at Rogan.

Rogan desperately whispered the words for another illusion spell, but without a clear plan, the magic fizzled away.

Roars of outrage went up, and the army seethed. Some ran. Others turned toward their leader, trying to fight their way through the brainwashed soldiers and hired mercenaries protecting him.

"You *bitch!*" Rogan screamed, wheeling his horse around. "I'll have your head, and your bastard father's, too!"

"*Charge!*" Bette screamed from behind the wall.

Ropes slithered down, tethered to railings, and men began to slip down. On the watchtower, George and Adeline quickly jumped to the ground, their fall cushioned by Jakob.

"This way, my lord," he said, ushering his girlfriend and her father away to safety.

Julianne lowered herself to the ground as fast as she could, not stopping to wait for Marcus before plunging into the fray.

She used her staff to block blows and leverage her way through the press of bodies. She burst into a small clearing, then was yanked back a moment before a horse kicked out, narrowly missing her face.

"Bitch's oath, Jules! Be careful!" Marcus pushed her forwards again as the horse turned and they scooted past it. "I told you, we should have gone around the back."

"No time," Julianne said. "I can only track him while he's surrounded by people."

She angled away to the left, then changed directions before swinging back around. "Dammit! He's being pushed back and forth." She ducked a swing from a sword, then flinched as Marcus stabbed the man with a spear, splattering her with blood.

"Pick a direction," he said. "And I'll clear a path."

Julianne reached out for the small space where a conspicuous absence of minds formed a tiny circle in the middle of the battle. "That way!" she cried, pointing.

Marcus lifted his rifle. A flash signaled the blast that threw men out of the way, and he grabbed Julianne's arm, dragging her forward. "Two minutes, and I can do it again," he said. "But it's tight with fighting ahead."

Behind them, they heard a rearick battle cry.

"Suck me balls, ye hairy goat scrotums!" A kerfuffle nearby erupted as men ducked and ran.

Garrett plugged through, smacking the last man in his way with the flat of his sword. The soldier yelped and cringed, ducking as Garrett swung it again, whirling the lady before thumping the hilt into a temple.

The soldier crumpled to the ground. Garrett stepped on his back, using the valuable added inches to scan the battleground.

"Where's that slimy mucker, eh?" he muttered.

Julianne sighed. "Garrett? We need a little help over here."

"Aye! Who do ye want me ta hurt-without-killin'? Or, who do ye want me to kill? That's the preferred option." He chuckled at his own joke, then stepped off his unconscious footstool.

"Kill the ones in heavy armor," Marcus said. "They're over-paid, angry, and mean. Leave the ones fighting them, they seem to be Muir soldiers revolting against Rogan." He looked to Julianne for confirmation, and she nodded.

"Just be careful," she said. "We don't want Rogan to die. Not yet, anyway."

"If we're fightin' through that lot, let me get me girl," Garrett said. He sucked in a breath, then screamed *"WHERE'S ME LASSIE? WE GOT SOME KILLIN' TER DO!"*

A whoop and a holler bellowed out from behind, and Bette flew over a soldier, planting her foot on his face to kick off and jump over into the small area Marcus had cleared.

"There ye are, ye handsome barrel of curls," she growled. Grinning, Bette twirled around to face a soldier who had followed her. Two thrusts of her sword and he was dead.

"Oops. Sorry, Julianne, I forgot we're not supposed to be killin' 'em." She winced apologetically.

Julianne kicked at the fallen man's thick, shiny armor. "I think that one's ok," she said. "But we need to head for Rogan. You and Garrett take the lead."

Marcus was an expert fighter, but Bette and Garrett were like heavy buffalo. They hurled themselves at the wall of men, chopping their way through, strokes flying in unison.

"They've gotten better," Marcus panted. He jabbed his rifle into a man's throat, then aimed over the rearick's heads. "Incoming!" he yelled, firing off another round.

They filled the emptied space and continued to push through. Julianne held her own, cracking heads and shattering knees with her heavy staff. Some way in, she paused, listening to something no one else could hear.

"He's close!" she yelled, pointing in the direction of the void she could sense.

They soon burst through, coming face to face with a cluster of scared mystics and a handful of ferocious guards.

'Lord George' stood in the middle of them, clothes muddied and hanging oddly from his body, part of a cloak draped over one shoulder, hiding his arm.

His guards attacked. Marcus threw himself in front of Julianne, pushing off a heavy mace and stabbing the man in the gut before turning to face the next soldier.

Julianne's eyes turned white as she summoned her power. She slammed into Rogan's shields and felt them buckle.

She pounded again, and his illusion fell away. She ignored the gasps from those watching as the kind-hearted lord was revealed to be his cruel advisor.

Julianne knew his shield was almost down. Just one more strike…

Someone stumbled in front of her, and Marcus jumped on him, shoving aside a spear aimed at Julianne. Rogan stepped forward.

"You'll never take me alive," Rogan hissed. He lifted his hand to reveal a long, thin sword. He plunged towards Julianne.

Marcus yelled. "No!" as he flung his sword out and felt it bite into the soft flesh of Rogan's belly.

"Marcus, NO!" Julianne screamed.

CHAPTER THIRTY-FOUR

Marcus marched alongside the two rearick as they carried out Rogan's body, wrapped in a torn banner that displayed Lord George's coat of arms.

The fighting was done. A few small tousles still flared up here and there, but for the most part, the soldiers had either dropped weapons when Rogan's deceit had been revealed, or turned on those so far gone that they still fought in his name.

The mood was subdued, despite the victory. Both sides had taken losses, and Marcus knew the day would be remembered by all. However, it would take a very long time to be known as the glorious win that it should have been.

"You want me to take the head?" Marcus asked Garrett.

"Nay. Ugly sod is balanced just right." Garrett sighed. "Bitch's britches, I'll be glad to fill me belly with drink tonight."

"Aye," Bette said. "Though I'll be glad to fill me belly with rearick." She winked at Marcus, who almost tripped over.

"Och, ye've spent yer life listenin' to soldiers braggin' about their shaggin', lad. Don't tell me yer suddenly squeamish!" Garrett said with a laugh.

Marcus snorted. "Sure, but the soldiers aren't usually *braggin'* *about shaggin'* each other."

"What difference does that make?" Garrett asked.

"Well," Marcus said, casually moving a little way out of Garrett's reach. "Bette technically outranks me, since George made her Captain. You're just a friend. What am I supposed to do when she starts complaining about how small your dick is?"

Bette let out a bellow of laughter. "*Ooh*, aye, he's got a point, love."

"He's got a… oh, you're a wee bitch aren't ye?" Garrett said with a growl. "Ye let me fill yer belly, and I'll show ye what a real *point* can do."

"Oh, *hell* no," Marcus said. "Not in my hearing you don't."

"There they are!"

Marcus lifted his head to see Danil running towards them, Polly at his side.

"You're laughing, so that's not Julianne," Polly said, panting. "We've been looking for you lot for ages. What happened?"

Marcus looked at her quizzically. "Why would you think this was…" He stopped. The color drained from his face as he grabbed the body from Bette and Garrett.

Throwing it on the ground, he tore at the banner. "Oh, you fuck, fucking, *FUCKER!*" he yelled. He threw his rifle on the ground, picked it back up, then pegged it across the field.

"Wait a minute," Bette said. "Who the fuck is that?"

The red-haired youth Marcus had uncovered looked nothing like the man they had wrapped.

"Why, Marcus," Danil said, wonderingly. "I do believe you just got mind-fucked. By your own girlfriend, no less."

CHAPTER THIRTY-FIVE

Rogan collapsed on the ground, exhausted.

How did the attack go so badly? he wondered. *Everything was planned. Everything, down to the last detail.*

"*Julianne.*" He punched a fist into the ground. "Bitch. *BITCH!*"

If not for his final act of magic, one that nearly burned him out completely, he would be dead. Or worse, strung up as some kind of humiliating lesson to those who went against the Temple and its master.

Rogan pulled himself up and stumbled, forcing his feet into a desperate, clumsy run. Branches whipped at him and vines did their best to trip him, slowing his progress.

"You might be strong, whore, but I fooled you in the end." He spat, allowing himself to bask in that one, small victory against her. *I'll go back to Muir,* he thought. *Start again. I haven't lost everything, not yet. I still have Donna.*

The sky darkened as the sun slipped behind a cloud. The forest clung to him, tugging at his feet and bristling in his way. Rogan shoved past the thick foliage to emerge in a clearing.

"What?" he gasped, looking around. It was the same clearing

he had fallen in earlier. He could still see the gouges in the dirt where he had clawed at the ground.

"I'm turned around. I must be. She can't get inside my head; I'm too strong," he panted. Despite his words, panic wrapped around his chest, squeezing.

"I wouldn't be so sure about that, Rogan."

The bushes parted and out stepped Justice herself. Julianne stood tall, robe billowing in the breeze, her eyes burning white like a fire lit by the gods themselves.

Rogan whimpered, trying to sink into the ground.

"For the crime of using mental magic to harm, I find you guilty." Julianne thumped her staff on the ground, and it reverberated through Rogan's bones, making his teeth rattle.

"For the crime of using magic to kill, I find you guilty." She thumped it again, and the earth shook.

"For the crimes of deceit, rape, torture, theft, and revolt, *I FIND YOU GUILTY!*"

Rogan fell back, screaming. A chasm opened beneath him, and he tumbled in, falling into a black eternity. His body jerked and spun, the wind whipping at his clothes and tearing at his hair.

He fell, shrieking, as two glowing eyes stared down at him.

You are mine, Rogan.

CHAPTER THIRTY-SIX

When Julianne went back to the field with Rogan trailing behind, wrists bound with a rope that dangled from her hand, the reactions were mixed.

Though she did her best to drain away the desire for violence, a few rotten bits of fruit happened to land on his face, and more than one person spat on him. Others ignored him and focused on his captor, cheering Julianne and whistling as she passed them.

How about an honor guard? she sent to Marcus. *I don't want an accidental spear slipping past to undo all our work.* She stayed on the fringes, waiting for him to gather some trusted fighters to help.

Then, to Danil, *I need you to calm the crowd. No fighting. No sudden moves.*

Oh, sure. I wouldn't go near Garrett, though. He's still fuming. Julianne could feel the relief in Danil's thoughts as he subtly checked that she was unharmed and safe inside her own mind.

Thanks for the heads up, she replied. *Everyone ok back here?*

For the most part. A few bumps and bruises, but no one on our side died, miraculously. Julianne felt Danil's brain tick over as he thought about that. *I think the worst of the fighting was near the*

Rogan himself. Not a single Muir fighter left, they all stayed to fight back.

Julianne hadn't anticipated that. She thought the civilians would take Adeline's request to heart. It warmed her to know they had such dedication to their city and their leaders.

Once the crowd was stilled, and those from Muir, Tahn, and anywhere between had stepped back to let her guards pass, Julianne led Rogan into the city and up to the watchtower.

Side by side, they looked out over the mingling group, Julianne tall and proud, Rogan cowed and hunched.

"Rogan," she said, loud enough that those close could hear her. "Tell these people what you did. Make sure you speak clearly."

"Yes, Master," he said, adoring eyes looking up to her. "I tricked them. First, I used magic to brain wash some of the soldiers and the household staff. I made them adore me."

"Why?" Julianne snapped.

"I wanted Muir for myself! I'm sorry, I'm so sorry I displeased you." He sniffled, but Julianne ignored it.

"Then what?" she pressed. "Tell me about the last few weeks. Begin with Lord George."

"I threw him in a dungeon. I cast illusions and altered memories to make people think he was still around, then I took his place. I wore his image and pretended I was him." Rogan hadn't taken his eyes off her. It made Julianne's skin crawl.

"And all this?" She gestured out towards the army waiting below.

"My idea! When Adeline escaped, I was so angry. I don't know why I wasted my thoughts on her, Master. You are the one, you are the only one."

Julianne's eyes flashed white and a bolt of pain shot down Rogan's spine. It wasn't excruciating—Julianne didn't believe in torture—but it was enough to stop his blathering.

"I told Muir she was kidnapped!" he cried. "I asked them to ride with me, to take vengeance. When you brought her to the wall, I made it look like you killed her, only, it wasn't her, and it wasn't you. Oh, Master, please!"

He fell to his knees, sobbing.

"And then you ran like a coward. You faked your death—did you kill that young man yourself?"

Rogan shook his head, snot running down his lip. "I made him. I gave him a sword and made him fall on it."

"Rogan, tell these people why you're crying," Julianne's said coldly.

He sobbed once. "Because I want to please you, my lady. I want it so much I can't breathe. I only want to please you."

"Do you feel remorse for what you did? Or understand why it was wrong?"

"Would it please you if I did? I will, for you." He wiped an arm across his face.

Julianne turned to the silent men and women below, They watched intently, entranced.

"For those of you who don't know me, I am a mystic from the Mystic Temple in the southern part of the Arcadian Valley. I am a mental magician just like Rogan." She waited for the gasps and whispers to subside. "Unlike Rogan, I'm not devoid of empathy or a conscience. In fact, one of the main tenets of the Temple is to care for our fellow man—to protect them from people like this."

She pointed at Rogan, and he cringed.

"I would give him to you, to let you exact justice…" A few men cheered, but the rest sensed more was to come, and waited. "Unfortunately, Rogan cast a spell that would wreak havoc if he is killed."

"Cowardly pig!" someone called out. Cries of assent nearly drowned out her next words.

"That doesn't mean he will live." She turned to Rogan and untied his hands. Quickly knotting the rope again, she looped it around his neck.

"Stand."

Rogan stood.

"Over there." She pointed, making sure she was standing back far enough that those watching could clearly see Rogan standing on his own, out of arm's reach. They had to see Rogan acted alone, to stop the death spell activating.

He moved to the edge of the wall, looking down, the wind flapping at his clothes. Swaying a little, he jolted in fear, but didn't step back.

"Please, no," he whimpered.

Julianne stared him down, then whispered one last thing to him, her words just loud enough to carry over the stiff breeze.

"Rogan, jump."

CHAPTER THIRTY-SEVEN

Julianne caressed the smooth tabletop. The knotted wood was worn from many years of use, so old it was almost imbued with the history of the small house it lived in.

"You know there will always be a room for you here," Annie said. Her voice was rough, and she didn't try to hide the red that rimmed her eyes.

Julianne smiled. "I'm glad to hear that, Annie. If Bastian really wants to do this, I'll need to make more than one trip back here."

"This school," Artemis said. "It will need teachers, yes?"

"Artemis, I told you. There's no room for a crotchety old man on our staff," Bastian said.

"I'm not crotchety!" Artemis protested.

Silence dropped, so pure Julianne would have heard a pin drop. Then, the entire room burst out laughing.

"Och, yer a shit and ye know it, Art," Bette said, wiping tears of mirth from her eyes.

"It's ok, Artemis," Bastian said. "I was only joking. We'd be honored to have you teach our mental magic classes."

"As long as yer not taking the fire-casting class yerself,"

Garrett pointed out. "Or ye'll have ta run the lessons underwater, so ye don't burn the school ta the ground!"

"What about you, Danil?" Julianne asked.

He was the only one who hadn't said anything about staying in Tahn or returning to the Temple.

He smiled quietly and shrugged. "I haven't decided," he admitted. "I've finally found something—someone—that makes me want to see more of the world than stone walls and drunk mind-readers."

Julianne reached out to squeeze his hand. "I'm happy for you, Danil. And there's no rush. Well, not much of one. We're not heading back for another two weeks."

She had to form a treaty with George, on behalf of the Mystic Temple. The Temple would pledge a certain amount of funding to Bastian's new school, and Muir would match it. The details still needed to be worked out, though.

"I'm glad we'll have those two staying," Annie said, nodding her head at the two rearick. "Be good to have some strong hands and level heads around, now we've got people coming and going all the damn time."

Bette had already received her official badge as the leader of the Tahn guard. The ceremony had lasted two days, and included Julianne, Danil, and Marcus's designation as honorary citizens, and an official welcome for Bastian, Garrett and Bette, who were staying in the small town.

Capped off with Jakob's proposal to Adeline, the ceremony had finished with a street performance by the theatre troupe, where Francis attempted to juggle fireballs with Trini and almost set himself on fire in the process.

Then, food, drinking and lots of music and dancing had kept them going through to the next evening. Julianne had snuck away halfway through, to take refuge in Danil's house while it was empty.

Marcus had joined her, slipping into the spare bed beside her and finally allowing her into his mind, wholly and completely. They had stayed there for several hours, though neither slept, and Julianne had spent the rest of the week with a pink glow to her cheeks that even Danil had to admit he had never seen before.

Julianne let out a long, contented sigh. "I'm going to miss it here. I almost wish I didn't have to return."

"You could abdicate?" Danil suggested.

"Sure," Julianne said. A yawn interrupted her before she added, "I hereby designate you as leader of the Mystic Temple, Danil."

"Oh, fuck that, Jules. Get your ass back there, now!" he said. More laughter circled the table.

"You all look like you're in need of a soft bed," Annie said, standing to clear the table.

"Oh, Jules has spent *plenty* of time in bed," Danil said. "It's sleep she needs."

Julianne threw a napkin at him, then squeezed her eyes shut as another, bigger yawn slipped out. "Oh, dammit. I do need to sleep."

"Shall I carry you upstairs?" Marcus asked with a grin.

"Last time you did that, you knocked my head on the doorjamb, you big oaf," she said, giving him a light slap on the arm. "I'll just lean on you. Really heavily."

Annie clicked her tongue and shooed them away from the table. As they all filtered out of her dining room, she finally let a happy tear slip out. One hand on her hip, the other holding a damp cloth, she knew that no matter who stayed and who left, she was richer than she had ever been in her life.

FINIS

AUTHOR NOTES - AMY HOPKINS

OCTOBER 16, 2017

Notes? NOTES? I can barely function enough to remember what words are, let alone craft author notes!

Here's the truth, guys. I am not a fast writer. Oh, sure, I can get up a fast clip and when I'm on a roll I take full advantage of it, but currently, my life doesn't lend itself to such nebulous things as 'peace', 'quiet' or 'sleep'. Though, I think that last one is an urban legend, I haven't actually experienced 'sleep' in what feels like years.

My kids are as crazy as I am, and that's pretty damn crazy. My three year old has a love of interruptions, emergencies, devastating messes and explosive creations.

And yet, I wrote this book, this WHOLE BOOK in 31 days. For me, that's bordering on a miracle!

I hadn't even realised I'd done it until I'd written 'the end', and it only happened because of you guys. That sounds like a load of shit, but it's not, I swear. There are days when I just feel like stopping early, like hitting the quit button and taking a weekend off.

When I feel like that, I go see the fans. Those really, incredibly sweet reviews, the eager posts on the Facebook page, the amazing, kind comments on my own Facebook page or website, or fan mail in my inbox.

Thank you to everyone who speaks up. You can't even imagine how much it means, or how inspiring it is.

Now, I'm not promising my next book will be out in 30 days, but I will promise this: there's no quitting. No early days. No weekends off, until it's done. I love you guys and you've all given me so much. This, I can give back.

Happy Reading!

-Amy

First, THANK YOU for not only reading this book, but also reading to the end, past Amy's amazing and heartfelt notes to read mine, as well.

So, I'm going to add my comments here about how you, the fans, help me.

I'm about to write 50,000 words in a week, I suspect. Why? Because of you!

Well, maybe not (but really *yes*) exactly you. But, the aggregate (and yet *individual*) you!

I've mentioned before that at times, I've used the positive reviews to keep me going. To go there and get some 'atta boy' for when I'm feeling particularly exhausted or down, sick and tired of being either tired or sick.

I am aware that many people think "Oh, you write for a living?" and then kind of shrug off the effort. It's ok, they have no clue what being an Indie publisher / author is really like. In fact, I'm aware that many spouses of writers have no clue what it takes.

Right now, I'm writing book nineteen in one series, I've finished book three in another (with a collaborator) and written

4 short stories for either my release, or anthology work and about 75 collaboration efforts in just under two years.

Further, we have built a relatively large (for Indie) publishing company / group while doing this.

And released fifty audio books.

None of this would have been possible if *we* weren't willing to dig deep and accomplish way more than we thought we could, and if *YOU* had not supported us day in, day out, for weeks and months. Reviewed the books, purchased the new ones, and kicked us in the ass a few times (with love) as we stumbled in our efforts.

Each of you, in your own way, are our coaches. Each of you are our cheerleaders and supporters. You exhort, you encourage, you push and you threaten to get out the pitchforks and matches.

Then, you cheer us over the finish line!

For some of us, it was a month of our lives to accomplish getting the story out. Others might be two or three months.

A couple are a few hard, hard weeks.

Either way, you are there to read the books on day one, post your reviews and invariably, as we rest our heads on the desk, our cramped hands in our laps hoping the ibuprofen helps release the pain from the marathon sprints to finish our words...

You say, "That was a GREAT Read!" Then, we raise our weary heads to smile as the responses come in from the latest release...

To then read the follow-up. "So, when is the next one going to be released?!?!"

That is when we hang our heads back on the desk and *weep.*

;-)

Ad Aeternitatem,
Michael Anderle

P.S. It really isn't that bad *(oh yes it is!)*

BOOKS BY MICHAEL ANDERLE

For a complete list of books by Michael Anderle, please visit

www.lmbpn.com/ma-books/